Bella Broomstick

Other books by
Lou Kuenzler

A Royal Disaster

The Dragon Dance

Bella Broomstick

MAGIC MISTAKES

LOU KUENZLER

Illustrated by
Kyan Cheng

Random House 🏠 New York

Text copyright © 2016 by Lou Kuenzler
Cover art copyright © 2016 by Nicola Slater
Interior illustrations copyright © 2016 by Kyan Cheng

All rights reserved. Published in the United States by Random House Children's Books, a division of Penguin Random House LLC, New York. Originally published in paperback as *Bella Broomstick* by Scholastic Ltd., London, in 2016.

Random House and the colophon are registered trademarks of Penguin Random House LLC.

Visit us on the Web! rhcbooks.com

Educators and librarians, for a variety of teaching tools, visit us at RHTeachersLibrarians.com

Library of Congress Cataloging-in-Publication Data
Names: Kuenzler, Lou, author. | Cheng, Kyan, illustrator.
Title: Magic mistakes / Lou Kuenzler ; illustrated by Kyan Cheng.
Description: First American Edition. | New York : Random House, [2018] | Series: Bella Broomstick ; 1 | "Originally published as Bella Broomstick by Scholastic Ltd., London, in 2016"—Title page verso. | Summary: After failing the entrance exam to Creepy Castle School for the third time, Bella Broomstick is sent into the Person World, where she is forbidden to do magic while being fostered by a non-magical couple who are unaware of her ability to speak to a lost kitten and use a feathery flamingo pen to cast spells.
Identifiers: LCCN 2018002217 | ISBN 978-1-5247-6780-8 (paperback) | ISBN 978-1-5247-6781-5 (glb) | ISBN 978-1-5247-6782-2 (epub)
Subjects: | CYAC: Magic—Fiction. | Foster children—Fiction. | Humorous stories. | BISAC: JUVENILE FICTION / Humorous Stories. | JUVENILE FICTION / Fantasy & Magic. | JUVENILE FICTION / Family / Adoption.
Classification: LCC PZ7.K94876 Mag 2018 | DDC [Fic]—dc23

Printed in the United States of America
10 9 8 7 6 5 4 3 2 1
First American Edition

To my family. You are magic!

—L.K.

I drew this with a stick and swamp mud!

Chapter One

I am a hopeless witch.

Everybody says so.

Especially Aunt Hemlock. She woke me up at dawn this morning just to tell me how hopeless I am.

"Belladonna Broomstick, you are the most hopeless young witch in the whole of the Magic Realm!" she said, poking me with her long fingernails as the seven warts on the end of her nose wobbled like fat green frogs.

I don't have any warts on my nose. Perhaps that's why I'm such a hopeless witch.

No nose hair

No warts

Smile

ME

Nose hair

Wonderful warts

Frown

Ferret smell

NORMAL WITCH

If I could grow just one teeny-tiny wart, I might learn to be good at magic.

I yawned and peeked at my reflection in Aunt Hemlock's magic mirror.

"Aha!" cackled the mirror. "If it's not

Belladonna Broomstick. Just look at your big brown eyes and curls. Not a wart in sight. Pathetic. What a hopeless young witch!"

"Actually, Bella, I think you're very pretty," whispered a spider that swung down from the roof of the cave.

I blushed. "Thank you." I understood every word he'd said. Speaking animal languages is the only thing I am good at.

Belladonna Broomstick's Magic Skills

Wand Work: HOPELESS
Spells: HOPELESS
Potions: HOPELESS   YIPPEE!
Talking to Animals: EXCELLENT!!

"Quiet!" Aunt Hemlock grabbed the poor little spider by seven of his eight long legs and dunked him in her lumpy porridge.

"Let him go!" I cried.

As if by magic (which it probably was), Aunt Hemlock's creepy chameleon, Wane, appeared on the kitchen shelf. Wane gives me the shivers. I never know what color he is going to be or where he will appear next. He's always spying on me and tattling to Aunt Hemlock. Right now he was disguising himself behind a jar of frog spawn.

"Yum! Is that spider for me, mistress?" he slurped, sticking out his long purple tongue.

"Certainly not!" Aunt Hemlock dangled the spider above her open mouth. "This one is mine."

"Stop!" I begged, but Aunt Hemlock swallowed the poor thing whole. "How horrible!" I shuddered.

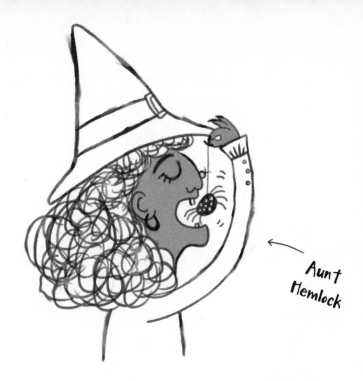

Aunt Hemlock

"And very unfair not to share," said Wane, turning piglet-pink in a huff.

Aunt Hemlock ignored us both and picked her teeth with a chicken bone.

"You're looking marvelously magical today, if I may say so, mistress," said the mirror, sucking up to her as usual.

"At least one of us is looking magical," sighed Aunt Hemlock. "Belladonna has her entrance exam for Creepy Castle School for Witches and Wizards today . . . but I don't suppose she'll pass. She is a hopeless witch, you know."

"Belladonna Broomstick is about as magical as mud," agreed the mirror.

I know what I'd do if I were good at magic. . . . I'd turn that vain, goody-goody mirror into a toilet seat.

I have never actually seen a toilet seat in real life.

Stinging nettles (ouch!)

But I know what they look like, because I've seen a picture in the Sellwell Department Store catalog—a wonderful, shiny book I found blowing around in a field one day. I have no idea where it came from . . .

perhaps the Person World? Most witches and wizards my age say there is no such place. But I keep the catalog hidden under my bed and peek at the washing machines and fridges every night. Even if it is only a fairy tale, it can't hurt to dream. . . .

"Hold on!" said Wane. "Hasn't Belladonna already taken the exam for Creepy Castle?" He gave me a nasty little smile. I began to imagine all the things I'd like to turn *him* into.

SELLWELL DEPARTMENT STORE CATALOG
Lizard-shaped salt shaker
(Page 183)

"Belladonna has taken the examination *twice*," sighed Aunt Hemlock.

I knew what was coming next. . . .

"And she has *failed* it twice too!"

"Third time's a charm?" I said, crossing my fingers behind my back.

"How hilarious!" The mirror laughed so hard it nearly fell off the wall.

"Not a hope, Belladonna!" wheezed Wane. His dry lizardy voice sounded as if he'd swallowed a bucket of sand. "You are your parents' daughter, after all."

"Don't you dare say anything bad about my parents," I said loudly in my best lizard language so that even stupid Wane could understand me.

Everyone says my mom and dad were no good at magic. When I was a baby, they turned themselves into white mice to make me laugh. It wasn't a very good idea—not in the Magic Realm, with so many witches' cats around (not to mention big, greedy lizards!). All that was ever found were two pink tails. . . .

That's why I live with Aunt Hemlock.

"Mom and Dad might not have been very good at magic, but at least they were kind," I said.

"Kind?" Wane's big, round eyes nearly popped right out of his head. "Fat lot of good that did them!"

"You horrible, leather-headed bully!" I picked up a wooden spoon and waved it like an ogre's cudgel. Wane shot behind a cactus and turned prickly and green.

"Goody," cackled the mirror. "A fight!"

Aunt Hemlock stepped between us. "This exam had better be third time's a charm,

Belladonna Broomstick, or I'll dip you in porridge and gobble you up like that spider." She snatched another one off the wall and swallowed it whole, just to make her point. "If you fail this time, you won't get another chance."

I wish I had a good pen to doodle with. This one is my favorite!

SELLWELL DEPARTMENT STORE CATALOG
Flamingo pen
(Page 118)

Chapter Two

The exam hall at Creepy Castle was in the deepest, darkest, dampest dungeon in the whole school.

My desk was at the very back, right next to Nightshade Newtbreath (worst luck).

"Hee hee," giggled Nightshade, showing off her perfectly chipped green teeth and sticking her (extremely) warty nose in the air. "I bet you won't even be able to answer the first question, Belladonna

Broomstick . . . or should I say Belladonna Broom*thick*?"

"Very funny!" I groaned. From the way Nightshade was laughing, you'd think I'd never heard her silly Broomthick joke. Nightshade is in my class at the Toadstool Spell Group, where little witches and wizards go before we're old enough for Creepy Castle. I have been there a long time, because I had to repeat the year—twice. Nightshade never lets me forget it.

"Look!" she giggled, pointing at Dr. Rattlebone, the ancient skeleton teacher who was overseeing the test. "You'll be as old as him before you pass this exam."

"I'm not that old! Dr. Rattlebone has been dead for nearly a thousand years," I said. "I'm only just in double digits."

Dr. Rattlebone rapped his bony fingers on the desk. "Silence, please," he rattled. "You may turn over your parchments and begin."

There was a swishing sound like a hundred batwings. I looked up at the roof of the dungeon, but the school bats were sleeping. I realized it wasn't wings I could hear—it was the sound of a hundred parchments fluttering over, ready for the exam to begin. All the other young witches and wizards in the room had done this by simply waving their wands at the page.

I scrabbled in my bag. My wand was a horrible old thing, with a terrible temper like an angry rat. "Ouch!" I yelped as a sharp splinter jabbed me in the finger.

I waved the wand at the page three times. (If you do anything three times in magic, there's a chance it might work.) Nothing happened.

"Having a problem, Belladonna?" hissed Nightshade.

"No!" I waved my wand again. One, two, three times . . .

POOF! A great orangy-red flame shot onto the desk.

"Help! Fire!" screamed Nightshade. "Belldonna has set her test paper on fire."

It wasn't only the paper—the big green bow in Nightshade's hair was looking a little smoky too.

I leapt to my feet, knocking over my chair, as everyone else in the room gasped.

"Spinning spiders, I didn't mean for that to happen!" I cried, trying to put out the flames with my wand. Unfortunately, that only made things worse. The burning paper spun in the air like a firework.

"I've never seen anything like this in over nine hundred years of teaching," said

Dr. Rattlebone, putting out the flames with his wand. "A very disappointing start, Belladonna." He shook his skull so hard that it fell off his neck and rolled past my feet.

"Now look what you've done!" Nightshade leapt up to return Dr. Rattlebone's head to him. "I don't think Belladonna ought to be in the same exam room as the rest of us," she whined. "She is far too dangerous, sir."

MY WORST MAGIC MISTAKES EVER

Vanishing Spell: Only my bottom half disappeared, but it was missing for a whole week.

Lizard Levitation: I dropped Wane in midair.

Turn-Yourself-into-a-Toad Spell: Unfortunately, I waved my wand at Aunt Hemlock by mistake.

"Try the first spell," sighed Dr. Rattlebone, balancing his skull on his bony neck. "If you haven't blown up the dungeon by then, I might let you continue."

"Thank you," I whispered, bending over the fresh parchment that had magically appeared on my desk.

TASK ONE: Using your wand, turn your shoelace into a worm.

I felt a leap of hope. I'd read up on the Shoelace Hex last night. I looked down and saw the floor crawling with fat pink worms that the other students had already made.

Swish! Swish! Swish! I waved my lumpy old wand up and down three times in a wriggly–squiggly worm movement. It was no good. My long brown shoelace was still trailing from my boot in a half-tied knot.

I was just getting ready to try again, when a scream from Nightshade made me jump.

"Belladonna, look what you've done!" she wailed. Curling his way out of her shoe was a giant snake!

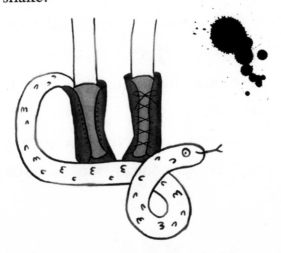

"Hopeless!" groaned Dr. Rattlebone. "Your wand movements were far too big, Belladonna."

I crouched down and hissed politely to the snake. "Welcome, friend!" He was a lot more exciting than a wiggly worm.

"Do something!" screamed Nightshade as the slippery snake slithered around her ankle.

Kaboom! With one wave of his spindly arm, Dr. Rattlebone exploded the snake with his wand.

"Poor thing!" I gasped. (Though I suppose it was only a shoelace, really.)

"That does it." Dr. Rattlebone's bony fingers grabbed my collar, and he marched me toward the door. "You have failed the examination!"

Everyone (even Nightshade) was deathly quiet now. My heart was pounding like a frog on a chopping board. "Please, sir, give me one last chance," I begged.

But Dr. Rattlebone shook his head so hard it toppled off his neck again.

"You have had your last chance, Belladonna Broomstick!" His skull rattled as it bounced across the floor. "You will never be a student at Creepy Castle School for Witches and Wizards!"

Chapter Three

"Failed?" Aunt Hemlock tore the note from Dr. Rattlebone out of my hand.

STUDENT NAME:

Belladonna Broomstick

Score: 0/100

Test Result: FAIL

Never come back! Ever!

Signed: Dr. Rattlebone (Deceased)

ZAP! She waved her wand, and the parchment ripped into a thousand tiny pieces. *ZING!* The jagged shreds of paper turned into a swarm of angry wasps.

Buzzzzzzzzzzzzzzzzzzzzzzzzzz.

No, not wasps—giant hornets! Each one had a stinger as long as a pin.

"Blistering bugs!" I ducked under the table, sure that the striped swarm would attack me. But they shot straight out the cave door. I didn't blame them. The mood Aunt Hemlock was in, she would probably turn them into a spicy hornet curry—stingers and all.

"What am I going to do with you?" she thundered as purple steam poured from her ears. "What use is a witch who cannot do the simplest magic?"

"I could l-l-learn," I stammered.

"*Where?*" Aunt Hemlock's green warts were wobbling like jelly. "Where can you learn to be a proper witch now that you have failed to get a place at Creepy Castle?"

"I—I don't know," I sighed. She had a point. Creepy Castle is the only school on this side of the Magic Mountains.

"Perhaps I could stay at home and practice my animal languages," I said. I can already make myself understood with nearly all the common creatures in the Magic Realm.

Lizard Lisp: Good
(only way to find out what Wane is up to next)

Spider Speak: Good
(plenty of practice in the cave)

Bat Shriek, Snake Spiel, and Owl Hoot: Not bad

24

 Hornet Hum, Frog Croak, and Toad Talk: Improving

****Cat Chat: Best of all
(my favorite language)****

"Talking to animals? What's the point in that?" snarled Aunt Hemlock. "The only thing those creatures are any good for is to be boiled up in potions and spells."

"Charming!" gulped Wane as he scuttled away from the bubbling cauldron.

"Belladonna could always volunteer at the potions laboratory," laughed the magic mirror. "The magicians could practice on her until they get their mixtures just right."

"That is not a bad idea." Aunt Hemlock's

green eyes sparkled. "Seeing as how you like animals so much, Belladonna, you could be a sort of guinea pig for the laboratory." She raised her wand.

POOF!

The air fizzled out of me like a popped balloon, and I shrank to the ground.

"Eek! What am I doing down here?" I peered out from under a coat of shaggy orange hair. All I could think about was how much I wanted to eat a carrot . . . or maybe a nice fat sunflower seed and a hunk of lettuce.

I stared at the mirror and squeaked. Aunt Hemlock had turned me into a guinea pig!

"Hilarious!" said Wane, laughing until he was plaid all over. "But I've got a better idea."

Aunt Hemlock sighed and waved her wand. "Let's hear it, then."

PING!

I turned back into a girl. I shook my arms and counted my fingers. Ten. I wriggled my toes. They were all there too. Phew! Fingers and toes are always getting left behind after a spell.

Everything was back to normal . . . except I still would have given anything to eat a nice juicy carrot.

"Belladonna should get a job with the trolls in the cauldron factory," snickered Wane.

"Belladonna *is* about as stupid as a troll!" Aunt Hemlock smiled.

"I wouldn't mind," I said. It's hard work at the factory, melting iron inside a roaring volcano. But my friend Gawpaw is a troll. He says that once the shift is over, they dance to tin flutes and cook stew in an iron pot as big as a bathtub—not that I've ever actually seen a bathtub except in the Sellwell Department Store catalog (page 73). Aunt Hemlock makes me bathe in the swamp.

"Trolls aren't stupid," I said. "Gawpaw knows—"

"Enough!" Aunt Hemlock raised her hand. "No niece of mine, no matter how hopeless, is going to work among those smelly creatures."

That was pretty funny, coming from Aunt Hemlock. She stinks of rotten eggs, garlic, and cheesy feet . . . except on bath night, when she smells of swamp mud.

"If you cannot learn to be a proper young witch, then there is only one place for you," said Aunt Hemlock with an evil grin.

"No! Not . . ." The mirror gasped and shivered on the slimy green wall.

"Surely you don't mean . . . ?" Wane peered at Aunt Hemlock from behind his two-toed hands. "Is that wise, mistress?"

"Where are you going to send me?" I asked. Surely whatever she was planning couldn't be worse than working inside a roaring volcano or being experimented on in a potions lab.

"It's perfect! I can't believe I didn't think of it sooner." Aunt Hemlock threw back her head and laughed. "Belladonna Broomstick, I am going to send you to live in the Person World."

"The Person World?" I felt as if a thousand fawns were leaping inside my tummy. "You mean, where the human beings live?"

Nightshade Newtbreath says only babies believe in the Person World. Witches and wizards tell their children about it to scare them and make them be good. There are strange stories about the Wart Stealer, toothbrushes, and the No-More-Bogeyman. But ever since I found the Sellwell Department Store catalog, I knew it was real!

"The Person World will suit you perfectly," cackled Aunt Hemlock. "There is no magic at all, and Persons are so stupid you should fit right in. After all, Belladonna Broomstick, you are—"

"A hopeless witch." I beamed. For once I didn't mind a bit. I was off to the Person World—the land of toilet seats and fluffy slippers. That was magic enough for me.

Chapter Four

I clung to Aunt Hemlock's waist as we shot through the darkness on her broomstick. "Hold tight," she barked. "We're coming to the edge of the Magic Realm."

"I'm holding as tight as I can." I gulped as my pointy witch's hat blew away in the wind.

"Don't worry. You won't be needing that again," she laughed.

Bam! Something cold and slimy hit me in the face. "Ouch! What was that?" I cried.

"The Curtain of Invisibility," hissed Aunt Hemlock. "It is drawn around the Magic Realm to keep the witches and wizards hidden from the Person World."

How could something invisible hurt so much? It was like being slapped in the mouth by a big wet fish. I struggled to keep my balance but toppled off the broomstick and began to tumble through the dark sky.

Just in time, I grabbed hold of the bristles on the back of the broom. "That was a close one!" I cried as I dangled in midair.

"You'll just have to stay like that. I'm not stopping," snapped Aunt Hemlock.

My arm felt as if it was going to be wrenched from its socket, but at least I couldn't smell Aunt Hemlock's stinky old cloak down here. "Are we nearly there yet?"

"I wouldn't be in such a hurry if I were

you," laughed Wane. He was riding in front of Aunt Hemlock like a dragon on the prow of a ship. "Persons eat witches for their breakfast, you know!"

"Scuttling scorpions!" I gasped. I could see a ring of bright lights glowing in the distance. Were the Persons lighting a fire ready to boil me in a pot? But I thought of the Sellwell catalog rolled up secretly in the bottom of my travel sack. Wane didn't know anything. The Person World was good and kind. . . . I was sure of it.

As we flew on, I realized the glow beneath us was just a line of tall lanterns twinkling in the darkness. "How pretty," I whispered.

"They're only streetlights," sighed Aunt Hemlock. I scrambled back onto the broom as we swooped over a signpost:

WELCOME TO
MERRYMEET VILLAGE
Please Drive Carefully

"Ha! Doesn't say anything about flying, though, does it?" she chuckled, looping the loop.

"Help!" I cried, hanging upside down.

"I feel broom-sick!" groaned Wane.

"What a lily-livered pair you are!" whooped Aunt Hemlock as we dive-bombed a village green, a duck pond, and snug little houses all around. She raised her wand and waved it above the rooftops, muttering a strange chant:

"Persons round this ring of green,
Let your secret dreams be seen!
Rise, foolish thoughts, and show the way
To where this hopeless witch will stay."

My heart gave a leap. This was the village where I was going to live. "Will your spell really show us my new home?" I asked.

"Precisely. Keep your eyes peeled," Aunt Hemlock cackled. "You'll know what we're looking for when you see it!"

I stared down at the sleeping village with its moonlit cottages. Brightly colored mist rose out of their chimneys and filled the sky.

Aunt Hemlock shook her head. "None of those are the dreams we're after."

We flew on over chestnut trees and narrow, winding streets. A burbling river flowed under a humpback bridge, and roses rambled over low stone walls.

It was the prettiest place I had ever seen—except for one big dark house hunched like a cold gray rock on the far side of the village green. As we flew closer, I saw high iron railings covered with sharp barbed wire that coiled like snakes around the top of the spikes.

Wane whistled. "Cool security!"

"I do like the bars on the windows. Gives it such a lovely dungeon feel," Aunt Hemlock agreed.

My heart plunged like a stone in a well. This would be just the sort of place Aunt Hemlock was looking for. I was sure of it.

Suddenly the courtyard was filled with light. There was a sound of a hundred locks and bolts being undone as the door swung open.

"Who's there?" shouted a man as thin as a wand. "I'll call the police!"

Police? I thought of the giant one-eyed Cyclops Cops who stamp out trouble in the Magic Realm. Would the Police Persons be as scary as that?

"Nosy busybody! I've got a good mind to put a hex on him," thundered Aunt Hemlock as we shot over the roof like a firecracker. My heart soared as we left the grim gray house behind. We weren't stopping there after all.

"Look!" cried Aunt Hemlock, swooping over the spiky fence and hovering above a birdbath in the yard next door. "This is the one! I knew my spell would lead the way."

I peered over her shoulder and saw an adorable white cottage with a thatched roof. Out of the chimney came a shining swirl of pink-and-silver smoke.

"Quick!" Aunt Hemlock whispered. "Where's my snare?" She dug underneath her cloak and pulled out a ragged butterfly net.

"Catch it!" cried Wane as the smoky mist swirled all around us.

"You can't catch smoke in a net," I said, confused.

But Aunt Hemlock hunched forward. "This isn't smoke—it's magic!" She pulled a small glass jar from her pocket and plunged it into the net. "Got you!" She grinned, slamming the lid on tight.

Aunt Hemlock held up the jar in a stream of moonlight. The smoke was gone, and a pale silvery moth was beating its wings against the glass.

Actual size

"The poor thing!" I cried. "Let it go!"

"Certainly not." Aunt Hemlock pointed at the pretty white cottage. "The foolish Persons who live here have a dream—something they have always hoped for.

I have caught their hope and turned it into this moth."

She stabbed the lid of the jar with her sharp green fingernails, making two small airholes. "Let's hear what it has to say, shall we?" She raised the jar to her ear. "Idiots . . ." she laughed. "Fools."

"What?" said Wane, grinning. "What do the Persons hope for?"

"Yes, tell us," I whispered, looking down at the cozy little cottage and wondering who might live inside. My heart was fluttering as fast as the moth in the jar.

"They hope," said Aunt Hemlock slowly, "for a child."

Chapter Five

"Fizzing ferrets!" I gulped as Aunt Hemlock landed the broom outside the pretty white cottage. "The Persons who live here want a child?" I watched the fragile hope moth flutter in the jar. "That's perfect. If they want a child . . . they might want *me*."

"You!" Aunt Hemlock snorted. "Who'd want *you*?"

Wane snickered. "Even Persons aren't that stupid."

"They hope for a child. That's a start at least. But we'll have to use very powerful magic before any Person would agree to take on somebody like you," said Aunt Hemlock, shaking the jar so hard the poor moth turned topsy-turvy.

"More magic. Of course." I sank down inside my tattered black cloak. "How silly of me." I could smell the sweet scent of the honeysuckle tumbling around the cottage door. It was the prettiest house in the whole village, with its wishing well on the lawn and window box full of flowers. In the glow of a lamp hanging by the door, I could see that the front door was painted sunflower yellow, and a mat on the step said WELCOME! I should have known it would never be possible for me to live in a pretty little cottage like this. Not without tricking the Persons with a spell.

"Disgusting little place, isn't it?" Aunt Hemlock shuddered. "Sweet as a cupcake. Yuck!"

"Revolting!" Wane stuck out his purple tongue and made a gagging sound.

But they were wrong. I couldn't think of anywhere I'd rather live. "Honeysuckle Cottage," I whispered, reading the name near the door. "If we have to use magic, then let's do it." I fumbled for my wand. "Ouch!" As usual, an angry splinter jabbed my finger. "Here goes!" If there was ever a spell I had wanted to get right, it was this one.

I'll just say what I feel, I thought, waving my wand in the air.

> *"Roof of straw and yellow front door,*
> *Be my home forevermore . . ."*

"What are you doing?" cried Aunt Hemlock. She spread her arms like a swooping bat and dived in front of me. "You're not allowed to do magic in the Person World—not without an examination certificate." She waved her own wand under my nose. "If you had been offered a place at Creepy Castle, you would have been trained to use magic properly. As you failed, you cannot use *any* magic ever again. Do you understand me?"

"Never?" A strange feeling of emptiness curled inside me—the same hollow thud I get sometimes when I wake up after dreaming about Mom and Dad. For a moment, everything always seems perfect—then I open my eyes and remember I'm an orphan and Mom and Dad are never coming back. "No spells at all?" I asked, swallowing hard.

"No spells, no potions, no chants, no charms, no incantations, no hexes," said Aunt Hemlock. "Hold out your wand and shout: *Adieu.*"

"A-dew?" As soon as I said it, the wand leapt out of my hands, wriggled in midair, and turned into an enormous brown rat with sharp yellow teeth and a long pink tail.

"Eek," it squeaked as it scurried through the fence, toward the cold gray house next door.

"So you really *were* a rat," I whispered. "I always thought you might be." But the wand was gone.

As I turned back, picking the last jagged splinter out of my finger, the hollow feeling inside me grew deeper. I've never actually gotten a spell right in my whole life . . . so it wasn't *magic* exactly that I'd miss (nor my grumpy old wand). But there was a feeling I got every time I waved my wand or muttered a chant. A little fizz of excitement. A tiny tingle of hope that the magic might just go right. I don't suppose I'll ever feel that tingle again.

"You will be a boring, non-magic Person from now on," said Aunt Hemlock firmly. "It really shouldn't be too difficult; it's not as if you were ever useful in the Magic Realm."

"Useless as a leaky cauldron!" said Wane, laughing so hard he flashed like a set of Christmas lights (the Sellwell Department Store catalog, pages 198–204).

They were right of course. But my heart was pounding—a magical life, living in Aunt Hemlock's cave, was all I had ever known.

"Stand back and leave the magic to me," said Aunt Hemlock as her wand spat sparks. "These silly Persons wished for a child. . . . Well, they should be careful what they wish for."

POOF!

Suddenly Aunt Hemlock was wearing a purple suit.

"There! Now I look like a smart business Person." She grinned. "All I need is a handy bag. . . . Ah, Wane."

"No, mistress, not me!" He ducked behind a flowerpot, but it was too late.

Pow!

Aunt Hemlock grabbed him by the tail, turned him into a lizard-skin handbag, and slung him over her shoulder. "It's only for a little while."

"Ha!" I smiled, but then she spun around and pointed her wand at me.

Ping!

"Dingley daisies!" I gasped. "I look like . . . like Gretel." I was now wearing a brown dress and an apron.

"Exactly! From the fairy tale." Aunt Hemlock beamed. "That is how Person children should look." She must have read me the story of Hansel and Gretel a thousand times when I was little.

"That poor, sweet old hag," tutted Aunt Hemlock. "Roasted in her own oven by those greedy children." She grabbed my shoulder and pushed me toward the cottage.

"Never let these Persons know you are a witch—not unless you want to be roasted too." She grinned.

She stretched her finger, with its long green fingernail, and rang the doorbell. "Let the games begin. . . ."

Chapter Six

A light flicked on in a window of the cottage.

"Coming!" called a sleepy voice inside.

"Smile!" hissed Aunt Hemlock, poking me in the ribs.

I nearly toppled over in surprise. Aunt Hemlock had never asked me to look cheerful before—she usually scolds me when I look happy.

"Persons like it when you smile," she

explained. Unfortunately, her twisted sneer didn't look very friendly.

"Can I help you?" A jolly-looking man,

as tall as a baby giant, stood in the doorway, blinking. "Yikes!" He took one look at Aunt Hemlock and jumped backward, nearly bumping his bald head and tripping over his enormous feet, which were stuffed inside a pair of very small, fluffy pink slippers.

"Ladies' So-Soft Cozy Toes—cotton candy color!" I gasped.

"What?" Aunt Hemlock scowled at me.

"They—er—belong to my wife." The man blushed.

52

"I couldn't find mine anywhere." He looked down at his feet and smiled. "I think I like these better anyway. . . . Mine are ever so boring and brown."

"They're perfect!" I smiled too (and not because Aunt Hemlock had told me to). I knew at once that I liked this funny Person with no hair on his head. I liked the way his shoulders shook as he laughed at himself. (Aunt Hemlock only ever laughed at other people.)

"Mr. Able?" Aunt Hemlock was grinning like a Halloween pumpkin. "I am from FAKE."

"Fake?" Mr. Able looked confused.

"I told you Persons were stupid," Aunt Hemlock whispered to me from behind her hand. "We are a charity," she said, talking slowly so that Mr. Able could understand. "F-A-K-E. It stands for *Fostering and Adopting*

Kids Easily. You and your wife did want to foster a child, didn't you?"

"Well . . . er, yes." Mr. Able scratched his head. "But we only called the agency yesterday. We haven't even had a meeting yet. They said it would take months to put everything in place." He turned and smiled kindly at me. "Although we would be delighted if things moved quicker than that."

"Well, they *have* moved quicker," said Aunt Hemlock, pulling papers out of her bag. "Much quicker. You said you'd be glad to take even the most hopeless case." Aunt Hemlock pointed at me. "Well, they don't come any more hopeless than this."

"I'm sure that's not true," said Mr. Able, frowning.

"You'll find out soon enough," sighed Aunt Hemlock. "Her name is Belladon—"

"Bella—just Bella." I stepped forward. If I was going to start a new life, I might as well start it with a name I liked. "I'm Bella Broomstick." I grinned.

"Pleased to meet you, Bella."

Mr. Able held out his hand. I wasn't sure why, so I just smiled even harder than before. "Pleased to meet you too."

"*Broomstick* is such an unusual-sounding name," he said.

"Not where I come from," I answered, thinking of how much worse it could have been.

Surnames at the Toadstool Spell Group

(of course!)

Addertongue   Frogfeet   Newtbreath

Batburn   Lizardlegs   Pustule-Pimpleton

Cauldronhead   McEggsmell   Vonvomit

Aunt Hemlock dropped her pile of papers into Mr. Able's outstretched hand. "You'll find these all in order," she said. "Now, if you'll excuse me, I must fly."

"But . . . hold on a moment." Poor Mr. Able stared down at the papers. Beads of sweat appeared on his bald brow. "This all seems most unusual. I mean, you turning up in the middle of the night and everything . . . I . . . I'll call my wife." He stepped back into the house and hollered up the stairs. "Rose! There's a lady here who says she's from FAKE something or other. She's got a little kiddo for us—"

ZAP! The minute he turned his back, Aunt Hemlock froze him like a statue. She snapped her fingers and leapt onto her hovering broomstick. She was already in her old witchy clothes again, and Wane was no longer a handbag.

"That was horrible," he choked, coughing up a coin.

"Stop moaning," said Aunt Hemlock, "or I'll leave you here in the Person World too."

"No!" Wane clung to the broomstick. "Anything but that!"

"Here! Look after this." Aunt Hemlock thrust the tiny glass jar into my hand and muttered an incantation:

"Take this jar which holds the hopes
Of these silly Person dopes.
Safe and sound the moth must stay,
Or its power will fade away."

"It's so *sparkly*!" I said, holding the jar up to the light near the door. I had never seen such pretty magic before—most of Aunt Hemlock's potions were gloopy and gassy like bubbling mud. But the moth's wings glistened with the dreams it had carried out of Honeysuckle Cottage.

"Careful!" snapped Aunt Hemlock. "When I trapped the moth, I tricked these fools into thinking they wanted a hopeless child like you. But if the jar breaks, the spell will be broken too. . . ."

"You mean, if the hope moth escapes, these Persons won't want to look after me anymore?" I asked.

"Precisely! You'd be no more welcome

here than you are in the Magic Realm," laughed Aunt Hemlock.

Wane giggled.

"And remember, Persons don't do magic— so there'll be none of your hopeless hocus-pocus either," snarled Aunt Hemlock. "If any Persons in this village find out you are a witch, they'll throw you into a dungeon. Then they'll start poking their wartless noses through the Curtain of Invisibility."

"Yes, Aunt Hemlock." I thought of the angry man in the big gray house, shouting about the police. Perhaps I'd be better off without any more magic after all. It had only caused me trouble. I took a step toward the warm orange lights of Honeysuckle Cottage.

"I think I'm going to like it here," I said.

"Ha! I wouldn't get your hopes up," cackled Aunt Hemlock, shooting into the sky. "You were a hopeless witch, and you'll be a hopeless Person too. . . ."

PING!

With that, she was gone. Not even a goodbye.

Before I could blink, Mr. Able leapt back to life. "So sorry. Strangest feeling," he said, wriggling his neck. "Like I fell asleep on my feet . . ." He turned and hollered up the stairs. "Rose, are you coming down?"

My legs were shaking like a bowl of newt-eye pudding. This was it—the start of my brand-new life.

I found a pencil! Look, no more splotches.

Chapter Seven

I stood on the doormat as Mrs. Able came bustling down the stairs. She was as round and rosy as an apple.

"What did you steal my slippers for, you silly noodle?" she said, swapping with her husband so that she had her own fluffy pink ones back.

I quickly scanned the sky, checking that Aunt Hemlock really was gone. Thank goodness nobody seemed to have noticed her flying away on her broomstick. I slipped the little shining jar safely into my frilly apron pocket, crossing my fingers and wishing with all my heart that the magic power of the hope moth would be enough to let me stay here.

"It's all a bit peculiar." Mr. Able was bobbing around like an egg in a pan of boiling water as he tried to explain the strange lady from FAKE.

"That may be, but don't leave the poor mite standing on the doorstep," said Mrs. Able, tutting at her husband. "Come on in, pet, before you grow roots out there." She stepped forward and gathered me up in a strawberry-scented hug. I didn't know anyone could smell so good—no rotten eggs, no garlic, no cheesy feet or swamp mud.

"It's Bella, is it?" said Mrs. Able, whisking me to a soft pink room that she said was called the den.

"Yes, Mrs. Able." I was so overcome I bobbed down on one knee, holding the frilly hem of my Gretel outfit as if I was meeting a queen.

"That's quite enough of that!" said Mrs. Able.

"Sorry!" I was worried that I'd made her mad. But when I looked up, I saw she was smiling harder than ever.

"Call me Rose," she said. "Or Rosie . . . or whatever you like. Just not Mrs. Able. It makes me feel as if I am in the waiting room at the doctor's."

"Eew!" I shuddered at the thought of the old witch doctor back in the Magic Realm, with his cave full of crocodile teeth and

YUCK!

pickled eyes in jars. "May I call you Aunty Rose?" I asked.

"Of course!" Mrs. Able's apple cheeks flushed pink. "Although I am not your real aunt," she said quickly. "It is important you understand that."

"Oh, yes!" I nodded hard. I already had a real aunt, and I didn't want any more of those.

"I'd better be Uncle Martin, then," said Mr. Able, holding up his left hand. "High five?"

"Er . . . " Yet again, I had no idea what I was meant to do. Persons were stranger than I'd thought. "High five!" I waved at him and wiggled my fingers in the air.

"Right!" Uncle Martin laughed and wiggled his fingers back. "Welcome to the family, Bella. We've waited a long time to meet someone as special as you."

"Oh, I'm not special," I said. "I couldn't even get into Creepy Castle School. Just ask Nightshade Newtbreath. . . ." But then I remembered I wasn't supposed to tell them anything about the Magic Realm.

"Well, I don't know who this Newty Nightbreath is," said Aunty Rose, laying her hand gently on my shoulder, "but you're very special to *us*. We couldn't have children of our own, you see . . . so we're bound to spoil you rotten."

"Rotten?" My heart sank. I should have known there would be rot and mold if Aunt Hemlock was involved. Though I couldn't see any. The room was spotless—especially the big shiny screen in the corner.

"Do you like TV?" asked Uncle Martin.

"Er, yes, please . . . but only a small portion," I said quickly. I hoped *TV* didn't taste like Aunt Hemlock's maggot-mush stew. Uncle Martin and Aunty Rose exchanged a glance, and I knew at once that I'd gotten it wrong.

"Pickled porcupines, I've said something silly, haven't I?" I blushed. "TV . . . *television,* of course." They were talking about the big black screen. I had seen pictures of screens in the Sellwell catalog (pages 242–259), but I had no idea what they were for.

"Nonsense." Aunty Rose took my arm. "It's no wonder you're thinking about food. You must be starving. Why don't I run you a nice hot bath while Uncle Martin makes you some breakfast?"

"Good idea. I'm starving too," said Uncle Martin, stretching sleepily. "Though I don't know why. It's still only half past five in the morning."

I glanced out the window. A pale late-summer dawn was creeping over the garden.

"It is strange you were brought to us in the middle of the night," said Aunty Rose as she led me up the stairs. "I'll give the agency a ring when their offices open."

I wondered if the agency was like the coven of witches who met every full moon to decide on new punishments. A terrible thought struck me. "Will the agency be able to send me away?"

"Don't you worry about a thing," said Uncle Martin. "The lady from FAKE said it would all work like magic!"

"Yes, like *magic*," I agreed, curling my hands around the hope-moth jar in my apron pocket. I realized Aunt Hemlock would hex the agency too. But suddenly I didn't care what sorts of cunning spells she had cast across the Person World—just so long as I got to stay.

Aunty Rose led me to a pretty little room with blue-and-white tiles and pictures of dolphins on the walls. She began to run clear, clean water into a sparkling-white bathtub. Steam rose up and clouded the window.

"Hot water!" I gasped. I was only ever allowed a real bath (rather than a squelch in the swamp) once a year—in the freezing sheep trough on Halloween.

"And a real toilet!" I dashed forward and peered inside the deep bowl. "What happens if I pull this?" I tugged at the little silver handle on the side. "Jiggling jellyfish!" I cried as a whooshing whirlpool swirled below.

"Goodness!" laughed Aunty Rose. She was looking at me very strangely. "How about some bubbles? Then I'll leave you to it."

Five minutes later, I was soaking in a warm, bubbly, peach-smelling bath. "Who says Persons can't do magic?" I grinned, sinking down so that only my nose was poking out above the foam. "Aunt Hemlock could learn a thing or two."

Chapter Eight

I lay in the bubbly bath so long my skin turned as wrinkly as a toad's kneecaps. "Don't you dare laugh!" I said, poking my soggy finger at the steamed-up mirror above the sink.

The mirror said nothing.

"Of course!" I smiled, drying myself on a snowy-white towel. "You can't talk, can you? You're just an ordinary mirror. Not a magic one at all."

I wiped the glass and peered at my reflection. For the first time ever, I was pleased I didn't have any hairy green warts on my nose. Uncle Martin and Aunty Rose didn't have any either.

"If only I didn't have to wear these silly clothes. They're definitely not right for the Person World," I sighed, climbing back into the Gretel costume. I slipped my hand inside the apron pocket, checking that the tiny hope-moth jar was still safe.

Then I flushed the toilet again (twice), just for fun!

Aunt Hemlock's spell must have been a pretty powerful one. By the time I came downstairs, Aunty Rose had called the agency. They sounded surprised but confirmed that all the paperwork to foster Miss B. Broomstick (me!) had been filed. Everything was in order. As long as the hope moth stayed safely inside its jar, I would be able to stay here forever. I did a dance of joy, and my frilly apron flew up in the air.

"I think we'd better get you some new clothes," laughed Aunty Rose, as if she had understood my deepest wish. "You can't wear that funny thing all the time." She looked me up and down. "How about a little shopping trip?"

"Shopping?" A thousand fireworks exploded in my tummy. "Like the Sellwell Department Store catalog?"

"Catalog?" Aunty Rose smiled. "We can do even better than that!"

"Breakfast first," ordered Uncle Martin, popping his head around the kitchen door. "Is there anything you don't like to eat, Bella?"

"Well . . . I'm not too fond of frog spawn porridge," I said shyly.

"Frog spawn?" Uncle Martin and Aunty Rose threw back their heads and laughed. "You are funny," they said.

Uncle Martin made French toast sticks and boiled eggs—not rotten ones like Aunt Hemlock cooks, and we didn't have to eat the shells either.

Aunt Hemlock's breakfast (yuck!)

Uncle Martin's breakfast (YUMMY!)

"Ready?" said Aunty Rose when I had eaten every yummy crumb. She grabbed her handy bag (as Aunt Hemlock would call it). "We need to go into town. That's where the fancy shops are."

"Jumping jawbones!" I was so excited that my feet barely touched the ground as we stepped out the front door.

"I'll stay here," said Uncle Martin. "I want to build a new birdhouse for my birds."

Aunty Rose raised her eyebrows. "He's bird-crazy!" she whispered. "Spends every minute cooing and clucking around the yard, as if he had feathers himself."

I smiled and turned to wave goodbye, when I heard a noise like a screaming banshee coming down the road.

"Sounds like a police siren," said Aunty Rose.

"They're heading next door to Hawk Hall

again." Uncle Martin pointed to the huge gray house I had seen last night. There was a screech of wheels and a flash of blue light as a bright white vehicle skidded to a stop outside the tall iron gates.

"A car!" I whispered to myself. "So they really are real. Look!" I cried as a tiny, terrified kitten darted around the side of the big gray house and scurried away.

"Poor little thing. It'll be in trouble if Mr. Seymour sees it." Aunty Rose pointed to a sign hanging on the spiky railings:

HAWK HALL
PRIVATE PROPERTY
KEEP OUT!

"Mr. Seymour does not like trespassers . . . not even cats," she said as the gates swung open and the police car drove through.

"Surely the poor little kitten isn't doing any harm," I said.

"No." Uncle Martin shook his head.

"Mr. Seymour claims he saw something flying over the village. . . ."

"Last night?" I asked. My heart pounded as I remembered how the man had shouted at us when we flew over on Aunt Hemlock's broomstick.

"Apparently he called the police right away, but they said he'd have to wait until morning," explained Uncle Martin.

"Mr. Seymour is forever calling them about something," said Aunty Rose. "He thought he saw an alien spaceship last week. And what was it before that?"

"A flying carpet," chuckled Uncle Martin.

I held my breath as two Police Persons stepped out of the car. Were they looking for me? Did they already know I was a witch?

But they turned to us and gave a friendly wave. I was relieved to see they had two eyes each and were only half the size of the giant Cyclops Cops back in the Magic Realm.

"What exactly did Mr. Seymour say he saw in the sky?" I asked, my tummy churning like a bubbling cauldron. The Police Persons might look friendly, but they still had metal handcuffs on their belts.

"Take a guess," said Uncle Martin, smiling. "You'll never believe it."

"Er . . . maybe a witch?" I squeaked. "On a broomstick?"

"Well, I never!" Uncle Martin nodded. "Spot on!"

"You're a smart one!" said Aunty Rose.

And they both stared at me in surprise yet again.

Chapter Nine

We left Merrymeet and drove to town . . . on a bus! The journey took ages, but I didn't mind. There were so many new Persons to look at, and not one of them had a wobbly green wart. (I tried not to stare at them *too* much.)

We wound along the country roads, past a big white windmill on a hill. I was so busy looking at all the different Persons that I almost didn't notice we had arrived in town.

"This is us," said Aunty Rose, stepping off the bus. "Stay close—I don't want you getting lost!"

I had never been anywhere so crowded in all my life. There were hundreds of Persons hurrying along the street. I felt I might be lifted up and carried away like a stick in a stream.

The tall buildings were big and black and as shiny as beetle wings. Then we turned the corner and I stopped as still as if I'd been frozen by a spell.

Ahead of us was a big silver building, seven stories high, with shining windows on every floor.

"SELLWELL DEPARTMENT STORE!" I exclaimed, reading the giant letters above the door. I gulped. "It's not just a catalog. . . . It's a real shop."

"Of course," Aunty Rose said, grinning. "Shall we go in?"

As we walked up to the big glass doors, they opened all by themselves, as if someone had waved a magic wand. "How did that happen?" I asked. But before Aunty Rose could answer, I grabbed her hand again. "Look!" I pointed to a large display in the window.

And there . . . right in the middle . . . was the fabulous feathery flamingo pen.

"That's my very favorite thing in the whole Sellwell catalog." I grinned. I couldn't believe I was seeing it in real life!

"It is lovely," laughed Aunty Rose, leading me into the store.

She had to keep pulling me along as I stopped to stare at all the wonderful treasures on display.

"There's the escalator," said Aunty Rose, and we stepped onto a flight of moving steps. "We need the fourth floor."

"Wondrous wizards!" Without even moving our feet, we were carried up to the children's clothes department. If we had been in the Magic Realm, I would have thought someone had put an enchantment on the stairs.

"You are going to need some everyday outfits," said Aunty Rose. "And some underwear and pajamas too."

I couldn't believe all the brightly colored clothes. Everybody in the Magic Realm always wore black and gray. And there were no cloaks or pointy hats here.

In the end, I think I must have tried on just about everything in the shop, but this is what we chose:

My favorite was the pajamas. "Can I wear them home?" I asked.

"Not in the street," said Aunty Rose with a smile. I was never going to understand all the rules of the Person World!

I put on shorts and a blue T-shirt instead. "Crazy crocodiles!" I said, jumping up and down in my new shoes. "These are the comfiest things I have ever worn."

Old clothes

New clothes

Proper Person clothes at last!

"Good," said Aunty Rose. "And what about this?" She pointed to my Gretel dress with the frilly apron, which was in a tangled heap on the changing-room floor.

"Hmm." I wrinkled my nose.

"We could save it for dressing up," said Aunty Rose. She smiled. "Or give it to the rummage sale . . ."

"What's that?" I asked. It sounded like the terrible mixed-up monster that lives in the bottom of Aunt Hemlock's well.

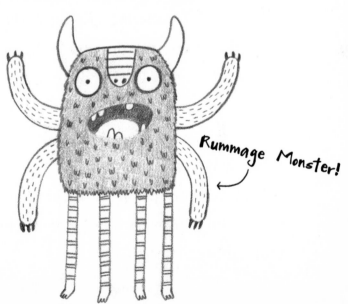

Rummage Monster!

"A rummage sale. Imagine not knowing what that is!" Aunty Rose looked at me strangely. "What a funny old life you must have lived," she said. "It's almost like you're from another planet." Then she blushed. "I'm sorry, pet. I don't mean to pry. I am sure you'll tell me more about it when you're ready. A rummage sale is somewhere you sell things you don't want anymore. There's a sale in the village today, to raise money for the Merrymeet children's playground."

"Great!" If someone else liked the Gretel dress, they were welcome to it. "I never want to see it again," I said, digging my hands deep into the pockets of my new shorts. At last I was beginning to look like all the other Persons I had seen.

"I'll go and pay and meet you in the café," said Aunty Rose. "There's just one more thing I need to do."

I stuffed the old Gretel dress into a bag and hurried to the café.

When Aunty Rose arrived, as well as the shopping bags of clothes, she was carrying a tiny pink paper bag and was smiling from ear to ear. "Now," she said, "how about some ice cream before we head home?"

"Laughing ladybirds!" I grinned, licking ice cream off my spoon. If only Nightshade Newtbreath could see me now. Here I was, sitting in the café at the Sellwell Department Store, wearing cool summer clothes and eating food so delicious it made my tongue tingle. Life in the Person World couldn't be more perfect!

Magic!

My drawings are about to get SO much better— you'll never guess why!

Chapter Ten

The bus stopped when we passed the old white windmill on the way home. A mother with a baby climbed on board, and two girls followed her. The younger girl was tiny, but the older one looked about the same age as me.

She smiled at me as she walked past, holding her little sister by the hand. She had honey-colored hair in pigtails and freckles on her nose (not a single hairy wart or green tooth, of course).

The whole family wore clothes with pretty patterns on them, stripes and stars and flowers all mixed up together. Their outfits looked nothing like my new clothes or any of the other things I had seen in the Sellwell Department Store. Some of the colors were a little faded, and there were patches stitched on here and there, but they all looked so cheerful it made me grin. The baby was dressed like a bumblebee, and I could hear bells tinkling on the bottom of the older girl's skirt.

"Come on!" she said, swinging her little sister onto the backseat. They all clapped their hands and sang a song about "the wheels on the bus."

I wished I were brave enough to join in—the two sisters were laughing so much. I thought about how much fun it would be to make a friend now that I was living in the

Person World. The smiling older girl looked a LOT nicer than Nightshade Newtbreath!

The singing stopped when we got near Merrymeet. The older girl pressed her face against the window as if she was looking for something she had lost.

I wished I could ask her what was wrong, but all of a sudden I saw the white chimney of Honeysuckle Cottage and the tall spiked fence of Hawk Hall.

Aunty Rose rang a bell. "Time to get off the bus," she said. "We're home."

I ran straight upstairs to my very own pretty pink bedroom with roses on the wallpaper. Aunty Rose said it used to be the spare room but it could be mine from now on.

I unpacked all my new clothes and put them in the chest of drawers. I was just hanging up my robe when Aunty Rose popped her head around the door.

"Leaping lizards!" I nearly jumped out of my skin. For a minute I thought she might be a Police Person coming to arrest me after all.

She smiled. "Sorry to startle you," she said, holding out the tiny paper bag she had gotten at the Sellwell Department Store. "But I just wanted to give you one more thing."

"For me?" I stared at the little bag. It was far too small for another shirt or a pair of shoes, and I had enough underwear and socks for every day of the week.

"Go on," said Aunty Rose. "Aren't you going to open it?"

"Can I?" I took the bag and peeked inside. "It's . . ." Suddenly I couldn't speak. My throat was too tight. My fingers were shaking like a dragonfly's wings.

"Oh, pet. Did I do something wrong?" Aunty Rose wrapped her arm around me. "It's just a small treat from me and Uncle Martin . . . to say welcome to our home."

"But . . . it's the flamingo pen." I held it up. It was fluffy and feathery and pink and perfect. "Thank you! It's the most wonderful gift I could ever wish for!"

"It's only a little pen," said Aunty Rose, smiling.

I stroked the fluffy feathers against my cheek. "It's the nicest thing anyone has ever done for me!"

"You poor lamb." Aunty Rose made a big, wet gulping sound like a foot stuck in mud. She turned away quickly, but I saw she had tears in her eyes.

"You should go down and show Uncle Martin the pen," she sniffed, pointing toward the yard. "I know he'd love to see it."

"All right," I agreed, wondering how I had upset her so much. But she wiped her eyes and smiled as broadly as ever.

"He's out there seeing to his birds, as usual," she laughed. "Not that there'll be anything as exotic as a flamingo in our yard, of course."

"I'd better show him this one, then," I said, waving the pen in the air as I dashed down the stairs.

"I'll pop down to the village," Aunty Rose called after me. "The rummage sale will be open now. There's just enough time to drop off that old dress of yours, if you are sure you don't want it."

"Positive," I shouted over my shoulder. I never wanted to see that silly, frilly Gretel dress ever again.

Chapter Eleven

Uncle Martin was standing beside the birdbath at the bottom of the yard. "Shoo!" he cried, waving his arms as I ran toward him. For a moment I thought he was talking to me. Then I spotted the same fluffy gray kitten I had seen running away from the Police Persons this morning.

The naughty creature leapt toward the birdbath and clung to it with one paw.

A flock of sparrows shot into the sky, tweeting in terror.

"Stop that!" cried Uncle Martin.

"You silly little rascal!" I hissed under my breath in Cat Chat as the ball of gray fluff jumped to the ground.

"Rascal! I like that name," he purred, puffing himself up to twice his fluffy size. "I think it suits me!"

"Well then, Rascal, just you leave those birds alone," I said, crouching down so that only the kitten could hear me. I knew enough about the Person World to know that it wasn't normal to hiss and purr as if you were having a real conversation with a cat.

"Shoo!" Uncle Martin charged toward the kitten, flapping an empty packet of sunflower seeds. Rascal shot away through the shiny black railings of Hawk Hall.

"No! Don't send him that way," I cried, thinking of mean Mr. Seymour. I ran to the fence and peered through. It was too late. The kitten had vanished.

"Don't worry. I expect the mother cat is around here somewhere. He's too young to be out on his own," said Uncle Martin, pouring peanuts into a feeder. "We can't look after every stray. No matter how much we might want to."

"No," I said. But my heart sank. Did he mean me? Was I a stray? Did Uncle Martin wish that he could shoo me away like the kitten?

I looked up at his gentle, smiling face and couldn't believe that it was true. He had only shooed away the kitten to protect his beloved birds.

"So, what's this magnificent plumage I see?" He pointed to the pink feathers poking out of my hand. I had almost forgotten I was going to show him the pen. "Has a far-flung flamingo found its way to my feeder?" He grinned. "I'll have to put out shrimp as well as peanuts if that's true."

"Ha!" I tried to smile. But I kept thinking of how it was all a trick. The Ables wouldn't even have taken me in if not for the spell Aunt Hemlock cast on them.

"Flamingos love to eat shrimp. That's

why their feathers turn pink," said Uncle Martin. "I don't know what these birds would make of it, though." He pointed to the flock of sparrows that had come back to the birdbath, flapping in midair as they pecked at a hanging feeder full of seeds.

The moment I saw their beating wings, I thought of the fluttering hope moth in the jar. "Dizzy demons!" The precious magic creature was still tucked inside my Gretel dress. It was in the frilly apron pocket.

How could I have been so stupid?

Aunty Rose was going to take it to the rummage sale. . . .

Chapter Twelve

"Sorry, Uncle Martin, I—I've got to go!" I stammered.

Aunt Hemlock had warned me to keep the moth safe. If the jar was broken, the magic would be gone and the Ables wouldn't want me anymore.

I dashed back toward the cottage. If only I could stop Aunty Rose before she left. "Hello?" I cried. "Aunty Rose? Are you still there?"

"You just missed her," said Uncle Martin,

catching up to me. "I saw her set off five minutes ago with a bundle of clothes for the rummage sale."

"Groaning ghouls!" Why had I told her I never wanted to see the Gretel dress again? I should have remembered the precious jar was in the apron pocket.

I darted to the hedge and peered along the road, but there was no sign of Aunty Rose anywhere.

Uncle Martin looked out of the gate. "Has she taken something of yours by mistake?" he asked.

"Yes!" I wished I could tell him what it was, but I couldn't. If he knew he had been tricked into fostering me, he would call the agency and send me away.

He smiled. "Don't look so worried," he said. "We can catch up with Rose in no time. She'll be heading for the rummage sale in the church hall, but she's bound to stop for a gossip at the post office first." He picked up the empty packet of sunflower seeds he had shaken at Rascal. "You go on ahead," he said, pointing down the street. "Follow the sidewalk past Hawk Hall and see if you can spot her. If not, wait on the corner for me. I'm just going to fetch my wallet so I can buy some birdseed while we're in the village."

He bustled back to the cottage as I dashed out of the gate, still holding my flamingo pen. The village road was completely different from the streets in town. There were no Persons anywhere . . . and no sign of Aunty Rose either. I hurried along the sidewalk beside the high railings of Hawk Hall and poked my head around the corner. Nothing! Just two fat ducks on the village pond.

As I waited for Uncle Martin, I peered

through the railings into the garden of Hawk Hall. There wasn't a flower, or even a single plant, anywhere to be seen. In fact, it wasn't really a garden at all.

I paced back and forth. What was taking him so long? I still wasn't sure exactly what a rummage sale was, but it didn't sound like a safe place for a delicate moth. If the jar broke, the little creature would fly off, taking its clever magic away forever. I was just edging a little farther around the corner, when I heard a tiny voice cry out in Cat Chat.

"Stop it! Let me go!" It sounded like the fluffy gray kitten . . . and he was in some sort of trouble.

"Rascal?" I cried, answering in Cat Chat. "Rascal? Where are you?"

"Ouch!" he wailed. "Help me!" His voice was coming from Hawk Hall.

I glanced one last time toward the village. Every moment that passed put the moth in danger, but I couldn't just ignore Rascal's cries.

I sped back around the corner and pressed my face against the iron railings. A tall, mean-looking boy, as skinny as a worm, was standing on the driveway and holding Rascal by the scruff of his neck.

Bow tie

Fancy suit

"Stop that!" I cried, shouting through the bars. "Put that poor little cat down!"

"Who are you?" The boy marched toward me, swinging the kitten in the air.

Shiny shoes

"I'm Bella Broomstick. I live next door," I said.

"Ah. The new foster brat." The boy wrinkled his pointy nose as if he had a horrid smell underneath it. "Daddy told me all about you. Well, I'm Piers Seymour, and my father is the richest man in this village. I don't have to listen to anything you say."

I remembered how happy I had been when the girl with the colorful clothes smiled at me on the bus. But it was obvious not all the children in the Person World

Person World bully

Magic Realm bully

NO DIFFERENCE!

were kind. *Bullies are just the same here as in the Magic Realm,* I thought.

"Can't breathe," choked Rascal as Piers squeezed him by the neck.

"Don't worry!" I mewed softly in Cat Chat. "I'll save you, I promise. . . ."

"You're strange." Piers almost dropped the little kitten on his head. "First you try to boss me around. Now you're talking to a cat."

"No, I'm not," I said quickly. I should have been more careful. I knew speaking animal languages in the Person World wasn't normal.

"I heard you," Piers laughed. "You were purring at him. . . . It was weird!"

"I was only playing around," I said. "Please. Can't you just let the kitten go?"

"He's trespassing!" Piers waved Rascal wildly in the air and pointed to the PRIVATE

PROPERTY notice on the gate. "Nobody trespasses on Seymour land." Rascal wriggled like a fish on a hook.

"He's only a little kitten!" I roared. "Put him down!"

"Make me!" sneered Piers, safe behind his high iron fence.

If only I still had my magic wand, I'd teach this bully a lesson. But the only thing in my hand was the fluffy flamingo pen. "If this were a wand, I'd turn you into a real live worm, Piers Seymour," I muttered under my breath, waving my pen in the air (three times). "That would stop you from bullying helpless little creatures once and for all."

Swish! Swish! Swish!

Poof!

There was a loud explosion. I almost fell

over backward as a puff of purple smoke shot out of the end of the pen.

"Galloping goblins! I didn't expect that to happen," I gasped. My fingers tingled as I stared at the pen in my hand.

It really *was* a magic wand.

Chapter Thirteen

Rascal dived through the railings and leapt into my arms.

"That was amazing!" he wheezed, still coughing and spluttering from being squeezed by his neck. "You saved me from the bully."

"But . . . but . . ." As the smoke cleared, I stared at the tiny pink worm wiggling across the driveway. "Look what I've done to Piers Seymour!"

There was no mistaking it—the worm *was* Piers; he was still wearing his red bow tie.

"You taught him a lesson, that's for sure!" said Rascal. "How does that thing work?" He stared at the flamingo pen in my shaking fingers.

"It . . . it's a magic wand," I said slowly, though I still couldn't quite believe it was true. "I waved the pen three times and . . ."

"Wow!" Rascal's big green eyes grew even wider. "You must be very, very magical," he said.

"Me? I'm not magical at all." I laughed. "I'm hopeless."

But my brain fizzed, and a smile spread across my face. I had done proper magic all by myself—and it had worked!

"That's the first time in my whole life I've *ever* gotten a spell right," I said, grinning. "If I'd managed that in the Creepy Castle exam,

Dr. Rattlebone would have been seriously impressed." Then the truth hit me like a charging bull. This wasn't an exam. My worm wasn't a shoelace. It was a boy.

The smile vanished from my face. "Now what am I going to do? I've just turned Mr. Seymour's son into a worm!"

I glanced up and down the road, but there was no sign of either Aunty Rose or Uncle Martin. Nor any Police Persons, thank goodness. If any Persons found out I had cast a spell, they'd toss me into prison and throw away the key—forever. The Ables would never want me back; it wouldn't matter if I managed to save the hope moth or not.

"Don't look so worried," said Rascal, rubbing himself against my ankles. "You were only being kind."

It was true, but I wasn't sure the Ables— or the Seymours—would see it the same way. The worm wiggled his head angrily from side to side.

"Can't you just wave your wand and change him back?" asked Rascal.

"I'm not sure," I said. "But I'll have to try!" My only hope was that Piers's worm brain was so tiny he'd have no idea what was going on. If I could just turn him back into a boy, he might forget any of it had ever happened.

"Here goes," I said, raising the fluffy pink pen. "Become Piers Seymour!" I said firmly, swooshing the pen in a circle three times.

Swish! Swish! Swish!

"Thundering ferrets! That doesn't look right." The tiny worm shot into the air with his little bow tie spinning around. "Sorry, Piers!" I cried as he began to loop the loop.

At that moment, an enormous black crow swooped over the fence from Honeysuckle Cottage. "Yum! I've never seen a flying worm before," cawed the hungry bird.

"He's going to eat Piers!" I cried, waving my arms wildly at the crow. "Shoo! Go away!"

Rascal dived back through the fence, spitting like a baby leopard. But the crow was almost twice as big as he was. He swooped down, opened his sharp black beak, and scooped Piers up in midair.

"Stop!" I cried, barking at him in Crow Call (which sounds like a hyena with a bad cough). "You can't eat that! It's not really a worm—it's a boy."

Rascal leapt in the air, trying to grab the crow's feet, but the cunning bird flapped higher. He circled above our heads with Piers hanging from his beak like a wriggly pink tongue.

"Drop that worm now, Mr. Crow," I cawed.

Suddenly Rascal stopped jumping and pricked his ears. "Listen."

Cats have very sharp hearing, but I heard it too. A soft purring growl like a tiger cub getting closer and closer.

I glanced past Honeysuckle Cottage along the winding country road that led toward town. Coming into view, at the top of the hill, was an enormous silver car as shiny as a suit of armor.

"That's Piers's parents," the kitten gasped. "They're coming home."

If I didn't manage to turn Piers back right

now, Mr. and Mrs. Seymour would arrive just in time to see their son being gobbled up by a hungry crow. "Be a boy again! Be a boy! Be a boy!" I cried, waving the pen.

Nothing happened.

The crow made a horrible slurping sound, and Piers disappeared farther inside his beak.

Chapter Fourteen

The Seymours' silver car was getting closer as the crow circled with tiny, wiggly Piers hanging halfway from his beak.

"Trembling toadstools," I groaned. "For the first time in my life I managed to get a spell right and now I can't undo it!"

Even brave little Rascal was panicking. His hair was standing up on end so he looked like a fluffy porcupine. "There must be some way you can turn the spell backward," he said.

"Backward? Rascal, you're brilliant!" If three swoops of my wand clockwise had turned Piers into a worm, then three swoops widdershins (which is witchy-speak for "the other way") might just turn the spell back around.

The crow took another loud slurp and swallowed Piers right up to his bow tie.

Swish! Swish! Swish! I waved the pen widdershins.

Poof!

There was a puff of pale blue smoke and a scream as Piers Seymour (the full-size boy) fell through the sky. The angry crow didn't have a hope of holding him in his beak now.

"What have you done to my worm?" he cawed furiously.

I ought to have magicked a mattress for Piers to fall on . . . or given him wings. Luckily, his jacket caught on one of the high spikes of the fence. He was left dangling like a piece of laundry pinned to a line.

"Eight, nine, ten." I counted his fingers and breathed a sigh of relief. None of them had been left behind in the spell.

Piers looked confused. "Who are you?" he roared at me as the electric gates opened and his parents' car pulled into the driveway. "What am I doing up here?"

Piers seemed to have forgotten everything. Phew!

"I'm Bella Broomstick," I said, scooping Rascal into my arms. "I'm just making sure this silly kitten doesn't trespass on your property. You know how naughty cats can be."

"Well, don't just stand there!" Piers

shouted, kicking his shiny shoes against the fence. "Get me down. This is an expensive suit."

His parents leapt out of their car and began running toward us.

"Sorry, I've got to go," I said. Rascal was laughing so hard I almost dropped him. I

felt all tingly inside. I had gotten myself (and Piers) into a horrible muddle, but I had gotten us out of it too . . . with *MAGIC!*

I almost wished Aunt Hemlock was here so she could see how well I had done. *Almost* . . . but not really. If she knew I could do spells she might take me back to the Magic Realm. I wanted to stay in the Person World forever.

Uncle Martin came dashing down the path from Honeysuckle Cottage, waving his wallet. "Sorry, it took me ages to find this," he called.

In a moment of panic, I shoved Rascal under my T-shirt. I didn't want Uncle Martin to see I was cuddling the same naughty kitten he had shooed away from his birds. "Stay there and don't scratch me," I hissed in Cat Chat.

But Uncle Martin wasn't even looking at me. He was gawking wide-eyed at the railings of Hawk Hall. "What on earth is Piers doing up there?" he asked.

"Er . . . I think a bird might have dropped him," I said truthfully.

"A bird? You're teasing me," laughed Uncle Martin.

But before I could say another word, Aunty Rose appeared from the direction of the village. Her hands were empty.

"My Gretel costume?" I cried. "Where is it?"

"Don't worry, it's gone to the rummage sale." She smiled.

"Gone? And the apron too?"

"I gave the whole thing away, just like you wanted," said Aunty Rose. She patted my arm, thinking she was being kind.

"Whatever is going on here?" she whispered as Piers howled like a werewolf and Mr. Seymour tugged at his dangling legs.

There was a loud ripping sound as Piers's trousers split in two.

Oh dear! mouthed Aunty Rose. Uncle Martin put his hand to his lips, but he was far too kind to laugh out loud.

"Don't gawk like a couple of goldfish!" snapped Mr. Seymour. "Do something to help."

"Of course . . ." They dashed toward the railings.

"I . . . I'm going to my room for a bit, if that's all right." I turned and sped toward the cottage, still clutching Rascal under my T-shirt. I could feel tears pricking my eyes. I glanced nervously at the clear blue sky, half expecting Aunt Hemlock to appear and whisk me back to the Magic Realm so I could be a guinea pig in the potions lab after all. Everything had gone wrong. I had made a hopeless mess of being in the Person World already.

RULE ONE:
DON'T USE MAGIC.

RULE TWO:
KEEP THE HOPE MOTH SAFE.

BELLA BROOMSTICK SCORE:
FAIL!

Chapter Fifteen

"Just stay under the duvet and don't go poking around," I said as Rascal hung off the end of my bed and tried to peer underneath it.

I knew I shouldn't have brought him inside without asking. But Uncle Martin didn't even want a kitten in the yard, let alone the house. No more strays—that's what he'd said. Well, he wouldn't have to worry about that for much longer. My Gretel dress was gone. The glass jar was probably broken already, and the hope moth would have flown away.

I could hear the Ables murmuring in the kitchen below. As soon as they escaped from the power of Aunt Hemlock's spell, they would realize they had never wanted to foster me at all. Perhaps they were already using their strange telephone thing to call the agency and say there had been some mistake.

Rascal stuck his head in the wastebasket. "What's in here?" he asked.

"Nothing!" I sighed. "I thought I told you to stop poking around."

"Do another spell," he said, pouncing on the bed as I sat playing with the feathers on my pink flamingo pen. "Do one on me. But I don't want to be a worm." He arched his back. "Turn me into a lion . . . or a tiger. It will be a very easy spell, as I am so big and fierce already."

"Really?" I smiled. I didn't want to tell him he was no bigger than a guinea pig.

"Listen to me roar!" he growled. It was more like the buzz of a bumblebee. "Go on. Wave your wand."

"No more spells!" I lifted my pillow and slid the pen underneath it. "You saw what happened to Piers."

"It was brilliant," said Rascal.

"He was nearly eaten alive by a killer bird!" I groaned.

"Imagine if the poor old crow had choked on his bow tie," giggled Rascal.

"You shouldn't laugh. We were in serious trouble back there." But I couldn't help smiling. It was impossible to be angry—or sad—for long with Rascal around. I slipped my fingers under the pillow and felt the soft feathers of the flamingo pen.

"No! I mustn't." I folded my arms tightly. "Persons do not use magic. And I don't want to either. Magic only ever causes problems. Now, will you *please* get back under the duvet and stop poking around!"

"Oh!" Rascal's ears drooped, and his tail sank between his legs. That's the thing with Cat Chat—you have to hiss and spit when you're being firm, but it makes you sound super fierce and angry. I must have sounded far more cross than I meant to.

"Mom always scolds me for being too curious," he mewed. "That's how I got in trouble in the first place."

"What happened?" I purred gently. "Where's your mom now?"

"I'm not sure," said Rascal, burying his head in his paws. "I climbed into a box, just to see what was in there. Then I fell asleep, and somebody carried it off. When I woke up, I was in a pile of boxes for the rummage sale at the village hall."

"Horrid sale! It causes problems for everyone," I said, stroking his ears and imagining a mean kitten-stealing monster wearing my Gretel dress.

"I wriggled out of the box and dashed straight home," sniffed Rascal. "But Mom had gone. So had my brother and sister. And the family we live with."

"Don't worry. I'm sure we can find them," I said.

"How?" mewed Rascal. "I peeked in the window of the apartment where we used to live, but everything had vanished. Even the furniture."

"Who'd want to make their furniture vanish?" I said. Persons really are very peculiar. "And how do they do it if they don't use magic?"

"I don't know," wailed Rascal. "If only I hadn't fallen asleep in that silly box. There wasn't even anything to see, just lots of dusty old books. But it was so dark and cozy."

"How did you end up at Hawk Hall?" I asked.

"I saw the broomstick flying through the sky, with you and the big witch . . . and the crazy lizard thing."

"Wane," I laughed.

"I wasn't scared. Not one little bit. I decided to follow it," explained the kitten. "Witches like cats, don't they? I thought the

130

big one with the pointy hat might use her magic to help me."

"Oh dear. Aunt Hemlock never helps anyone," I said, stroking his fluffy head.

"That lizard stuck his tongue out at me," said Rascal.

He looked so sad—ever since he had started to talk about his mom, all the puff and fluff had gone out of him. But what could I do?

"I wish I could help. But I don't even know your real name," I said as he curled up on my lap.

"It's Rascal now," he said, yawning. "You chose it. I never had a proper name before I met you. Mom just calls me Number Three, because she says I am smaller than my brother and sister . . . but I'm not!"

"Well, Rascal certainly suits you," I said.

"That's because I'm fearless and not afraid

of trouble," said the tiny kitten, yawning again. "Since you've given me a name, you'll have to help me. Mom says that's what naming a cat means. . . . It's like a promise to look after me."

"But—"

"You are going to help me find her, aren't you?" he said with a happy little snuffling sound. "I knew you would. Do you think you'll use magic? It'll be awesome if you do."

"No magic! I already told you," I said firmly.

But Rascal closed his eyes and laid his head on my knee. He was just starting to snore, when there was a knock on my bedroom door.

"This is it," I whispered. "The Ables have realized they were tricked by magic. Now they've come to tell me to leave."

Chapter Sixteen

"Bella?" Aunty Rose rapped on the door firmly.

"One minute," I called. I scrambled to my feet and slipped sleepy Rascal into my half-open sock drawer. "Stay there and don't move," I warned him. Then I opened my bedroom door to face Aunty Rose.

She was holding out a tall glass of something dark and fizzy. The only bubbly black liquid I know is swamp gas, which goes into most of Aunt Hemlock's favorite potions. Surely Aunty Rose wouldn't make me drink anything like that. . . .

"I brought you a glass of cola," she said. Cola? Well, that didn't sound too bad. . . .

"And some chips," she said, handing me a little snack on a plate. "Don't get any crumbs on the bed . . . and we're going to have to start eating a bit more healthy tomorrow."

"Tomorrow?" I gasped. So they weren't

sending me away? At least not yet. Aunty
Rose was still being so kind, bringing me
treats. Perhaps there was a chance the jar
hadn't broken . . . the moth was still safe.
"Thank you." I sniffed the bubbling black
liquid and took a tiny sip. "Fuzzy fungus!"
The fizz went right up my nose, but it
was delicious—like shooting stars and sugar.
"Yum!" I took a giant gulp.

"Careful!" Aunty Rose patted me on the
back. When I finally finished spluttering, I
cleared my throat.

"What would somebody do if they sent
something to the rummage sale by mistake?"
I asked.

"This is about that dress of yours, isn't
it?" said Aunty Rose, sitting down on the
bed beside me.

"Yes," I mumbled. I couldn't bear to make
her feel bad for giving the Gretel dress away.

I was the one who had told her to get rid of it in the first place. She wouldn't have known I'd left a jar of powerful magic inside the apron pocket.

"There's a good chance it might not have been sold," said Aunty Rose. "Uncle Martin can take you down to the village right now, if you like. He still wants to buy birdseed. But you'd better be quick." She glanced at her watch. "The rummage sale closes in fifteen minutes."

The rummage sale smelled like Aunt Hemlock's socks. But it was really fun and colorful too. There were piles of clothes and tables of teapots, cups and plates, a barrel of toys, and a basket of rain boots in every shade of the rainbow (though none of them seemed to make a matching pair). Nothing was shiny and crisp and new (like the things at Sellwell Department Store), but everything seemed as if it had once been loved. Jars of buttons and bottles of beads shimmered like treasure, and there were weird things too—a wastebasket shaped like an elephant's foot (Aunt Hemlock would have snapped that up) and a giant purple teddy bear as tall as Uncle Martin.

There was a table of tea and coffee, cakes and cookies and bright orange squash as well. Aunty Rose had given me a shiny half-dollar that I would have loved to spend on a giant slice of sponge cake stuffed with strawberries and cream, but I had to save the money to buy my Gretel costume back.

"Excuse me," I said, peering over a mountain of winter hats and woolly scarves.

"Hello, dearie," said the woman running the clothes stall. She was tiny and wrinkly, as if she might have tumbled out of a bag along with old clothes. Her kind brown eyes were as big and round as buttons. "What can I do for you?"

"Well—"

"How about a winter scarf?" She pulled a bright red one from the very bottom of the pile. All the others tumbled to the floor in an avalanche of wool and pom-poms. "It's summer now, but you'll be glad of something cozy come wintertime."

"No thanks," I said, scrabbling on the floor and piling mittens and gloves back onto the table. "I'm looking for a special outfit. Like a costume."

"Ah!" She began to flick through a rack of clothes. "Cinderella, Belle, Minnie Mouse, Mickey Mouse, a Dalmatian, Shrek?"

"No, it's—"

"Santa Claus, Elsa, Superman, Spider-Man—no idea what this one is supposed to be—a witch, a wizard, Alice in Wonderland, or—"

"Sorry!" I stood on tiptoe and shouted as loudly as I could. "It's a special costume I'm looking for, you see. Like Gretel from the fairy tale . . . brown with a frilly apron on the top."

"Well, blow me down!" She grinned. "Rose Able came in earlier and donated one just like that."

"That's it!" I cried, holding out my half-dollar. "Please, may I buy it back?"

"Sorry!" Her face crumpled like a paper bag. "You just missed it."

"Missed it?" The coin almost slipped from my fingers. "You mean it's been sold?"

"That's the rummage sale for you," she sighed. "Hundreds of things that nobody wants and one thing they're all after. Had the same trouble with a clock shaped like a fried egg last year. Mrs. Brimblecombe from the post office got quite nasty—"

"The costume," I said, darting around the side of the table so that I could see her better. "Please, it's really important. I don't suppose you noticed, but did it have anything in the pocket?"

"The pocket?"

"Yes."

"The apron pocket?"

"Yes." I felt a surge of hope. Maybe she had seen the jar and kept it safe.

"Sorry, couldn't say."

"Oh!" I sighed.

"I wish I could help, but I only had the dress a few minutes, dearie," she explained. "Rose Able had only just dropped it off, when the little girl came up. Desperate to have it, she was."

"Little girl?" I asked.

"Young Gretel. She's just four years old. Her mom used to run the secondhand bookshop." The woman smiled. "Gretel's her real name—just like in the story. Perhaps that's why she wanted the costume so much."

"I suppose that makes sense," I said, nodding.

"Don't tell anyone, but I let her have it for free," she whispered, leaning forward and taking my hand. "Seemed the least I could do after all the trouble that poor family has had. Mr. Seymour throwing them out of their home like that . . ."

"Mr. Seymour?" I asked. "What did he do?"

"He owns the building the family was renting," the woman explained. "But he closed the bookshop down and threw them out of the apartment with just one day's notice. He's going to turn the whole place into fancy offices for his concrete-making company, Seymour Cement. Now we don't have our lovely old bookshop anymore."

"That's terrible," I said. The more I heard about the Seymours, the more they reminded me of Aunt Hemlock and her horrid tricks. I wouldn't be surprised if they grew big green warts on the ends of their noses.

Piers

Mr. Seymour

"And little Gretel and her family have had to leave Merrymeet for good," she sighed.

"You mean they don't even live in the village anymore?" I asked. My last chance of finding the costume and saving the hope moth was gone.

"They only popped back this morning because they were looking for a lost kitten," she answered.

"A kitten?" My heart was racing again.

"They dropped off some books and things," said the woman. "They think the little gray kitten might have crawled into—"

"Into the box," I cried, flinging my arms around her neck. These were Rascal's owners for sure. "Please. You have to tell me where they've gone."

"That's easy. They've taken shelter in the old windmill. Dreadful, drafty place. Can't miss it," she said. "Five miles out of the village on top of the hill."

"I've seen it!" I said. "On the road to town."

"That's the one," she said. "Run quick and you might even catch the last bus!"

Chapter Seventeen

"Why can't we go to the windmill right now?" asked Rascal, scratching his claws on the end of my bed. "You could save your magic butterfly, and I could see my mom."

"It's a moth," I sighed. "And it's Saturday night, which means there aren't any buses until Monday morning. I missed the last one by a weasel's whisker."

I paced up and down the room. I wished I could help Rascal, and I couldn't bear the thought of waiting the whole weekend before I could try to rescue the hope moth.

The lady at the rummage sale had said Gretel was only four years old. She'd be sure to break the jar or lose it somewhere by Monday.

"If only I could ask the Ables to help," I said, peering out of the window as the last of the day's sun began to fade. "But then I'd have to explain how I brought you into the house without asking." Rascal curled himself around my ankles. "Then they'd get mad and throw us both out."

"But you are a witch," purred Rascal. "Couldn't we just fly to the windmill by broomstick?"

"No!" I said. "No more magic! Anyway, Aunty Rose probably doesn't even have a broomstick." The closest thing I'd seen was a vacuum cleaner.

"She does," said Rascal. "It's next to the mop in the back of the cupboard beside the stove."

"You've been poking around downstairs!" I cried. "What if you'd been caught? I told you to stay hidden."

"Sorry." Rascal looked up at me with his big green eyes. "I just don't want Mom to worry about where I've gone. I never even got to say goodbye to her."

"All right, all right!" I said as he rubbed his head underneath my chin and mewed pitifully. "Anything to get you back home before you cause any real trouble. How long was the broom handle? Do you think we'll both fit?"

Aunty Rose and Uncle Martin had tucked me into bed hours ago. The cottage was quiet and the yard was dark as Rascal and I slipped out onto the lawn.

"Ready?" I whispered, laying Aunty

Rose's red broom down on the grass. "Keep out of the way and don't ask any questions."

"Why would I ask questions?" asked Rascal.

"That *is* a question!" I giggled. "Just stand behind me and don't move until I say so. Getting a broomstick to fly is a very tricky spell."

This wasn't true, actually. Most witches do it about ten times a day, but I'd never been able to make it happen. Not once!

Things would be different now, I told myself, taking the magical feathery pen from behind my ear. My wand wasn't a grumpy old rat anymore—it was a beautiful pink flamingo. "If I can turn Piers Seymour into a wiggly worm and back again, I can make a broomstick fly."

"How fast will we go?" asked Rascal. "Will we be able to touch the moon?"

"Shh!" I held my flamingo wand above

the broomstick and muttered the words I had heard other witches say a thousand times:

"Sweep like wings into the sky,
Brush the clouds and fly, fly, fl—"

Poof!

There was a puff of pink smoke, and I shot backward onto the lawn. Rascal, who had been standing right behind me, tumbled too. We rolled across the grass in a tangle of arms, legs, and a fluffy tail. "Ouch!" I cried as his claw went up my nose (though I'm sure he didn't mean to scratch me).

"Did it work?" said Rascal, staggering to his feet. "Are we going to fly now?"

I stared at the broomstick lying flat on the grass. "I'm sorry," I groaned. I knew how much Rascal wanted to see his mom.

"We're not going anywhere." I was still as hopeless at magic as ever.

"Oh! Have you seen your fluffy wand-thingy?" asked Rascal.

"No," I said, scrambling around on the dark grass trying to find the pen. "I must have dropped it somewhere. . . ."

"No. I mean, have you *seen* it? Behind you!" said Rascal. His tail was puffed up to twice its normal size.

Very, *very* slowly, I turned my head. A large pink flamingo—a *real* one—was balancing on one leg, dipping her beak into the birdbath on the edge of the lawn.

"Fluttering feathers! Hello," I gasped,

reaching out to stroke the bird's pink plumage. She was beautiful. My broomstick spell might not have worked, but something much more extraordinary had happened instead. "I suppose if my old wooden wand was an angry rat, there is no reason my pen-wand shouldn't be a real flamingo."

"*Ark!*" squawked the bird.

"Shh!" I put my finger to my lips as a light flickered on in Hawk Hall.

"What's the big birdy-thing saying?" asked Rascal.

"I'm not sure." The bird stretched out her long neck, and I stroked the smooth feathers on top of her head. "I don't speak Flamingo." There aren't any beautiful pink birds in the Magic Realm . . . just crows and owls.

"*Ark!*" The flamingo flapped her wings.

"I think she wants to fly," I said. But she

bent her knees and tugged at my sleeve with her black-tipped beak. She scooped up Rascal, like a pea on a spoon, and swung him onto her back. "She wants us to come with her." I grinned.

"Is she our broomstick?" purred Rascal.

"Yes!" I cried, scrambling onto the flamingo's feathery back as bright lights blazed on all across the concrete gardens of Hawk Hall. "Fly! Fly! Fly!"

Chapter Eighteen

Rascal perched on the flamingo's back as we flew over the shadowy fields.

"Don't dig your claws in or you'll hurt her," I said, gripping the bird gently with my knees. I glanced over my shoulder and saw the flamingo's thin pink legs pointing straight out behind us. She was as long and fast as any broom.

"Crazy comets, this is amazing," I exclaimed as the flamingo shot through the air like a spear. "Every witch should get one!" It was much easier—and far more fun—to ride a fluttering feathery bird than a slippery wooden broomstick.

"There it is," I cried, pointing to the tall white windmill as the flamingo swooped over a line of trees. A swaying lantern hung in the porch, guiding us across the fields like a lighthouse at sea.

Even before we landed, I could see the dark shadow of a jet-black cat staring up at the sky. "Mom!" called Rascal, leaping off the flamingo's back.

"Careful!" I warned, but his mother didn't even wait for him to land.

"Where've you been, Number Three?" she hissed, pawing him on the ears. "I've been worried out of my nine lives."

The flamingo skidded to a stop. I climbed down and patted her neck. "Thank you for bringing us here!" I whispered, wishing she could understand me in the way Rascal could.

His mother had already stopped hissing. Her anger and worry were gone, and she was licking him, purring with love and relief as he explained everything that had happened since he first climbed into the box of old books. "You and your curiosity!" she sighed.

I smiled, happy we had returned him to her so easily. But I was sad too at having to say goodbye. I would miss the brave, inquisitive little kitten.

Just as I was clearing my throat to wish him good luck, his mother turned to me. Her fiery orange eyes glistened in the darkness. "So my boy's to be a witch's cat, now, is he?" she purred. "I couldn't be more proud. My own great-grandmother was a witch's companion. Greatest honor any cat can have."

"Oh, no, you don't understand," I said quickly, purring politely in my smoothest Cat Chat. "Rascal—I mean, Number Three—can't stay with me, Mrs. Cat. I was just bringing him home to you and his Person family."

"The family can't keep him. They don't know what is going to happen now that their shop has been closed down," said the cat. "They wanted to find him and check that he was safe, but he'll need a new home for sure. They've already given Number Two to an old man in the village. They're only keeping Number One because he's big and strong and can catch mice and rats."

"I can catch rats," said Rascal proudly. "There's a huge one behind the trash cans at Hawk Hall. I pounced on it once, but it bit my tail off and turned into a puff of black smoke."

"Oh dear," I laughed. "I don't think that's an ordinary rat—it sounds like my grumpy old wand. I told you it ran away."

"Brave boy. You are ready to leave home," said Rascal's mother. "You will make a fine magic cat—I knew your eyes are as green as emeralds for a reason. All witches' cats have green eyes, you know." Her own fiery eyes sparkled. "Go with Miss Bella. Help her with her spells and ride the skies on a broomstick or . . ." She looked at the flamingo and shook her head in confusion. "Or a big pink bird, at any rate."

"I will." Rascal puffed himself up with pride as Mrs. Cat straightened his whiskers. "I'll be the best witch's cat ever."

"But . . . you can't live with me," I said.

I felt as if I were pelting the tiny kitten with stones. "You know I'd love to take you home, more than anything. But the Ables won't let me have a cat."

"Oh!" Rascal made a tiny mewing sound halfway between a sniff and a cough. "Doesn't matter. I'm very busy here anyway," he said. "I have rats and mice to catch. . . ." Then he turned away without another word and hung his head low. I'd never heard him so silent before. I would rather he hissed and scratched at me than this.

"You named him," said his mother. "That means he's bonded to you now."

"I'm sorry." I shook my head. "He'll find a lovely new home again in no time. . . . He's . . . well, he's very cute." I knew that would go to Rascal's head. But it was true; there must be hundreds of Persons who'd want an adorable little kitten like him.

"I have brought you here safely," I said, blowing Rascal a kiss. "But now I have to find the hope moth and get back to Honeysuckle Cottage."

I took a step toward the windmill. Out of the corner of my eye, I saw Rascal creep forward as if to follow me.

"Shoo!" I hissed, clapping my hands at him, although I felt as if my heart were going to break.

"Come along, Number Three!" His mother stalked off into the darkness.

"My name is Rascal!" he said, arching his back like a lion cub as he followed her into the gloom.

"Yes, it is! You'll always be Rascal to me," I called after him.

But before I could hear his answer, the door to the windmill swung open and a small child stood yawning in the moonlight. My heart leapt.

I knew her. It was the little girl from the bus—the one whose big sister smiled at me. They had clapped their hands and sung about wheels on the bus together.

"Gretel," I whispered, crouching down so that I was the same height she was. "Hello."

She was wearing my brown dress and the (very) frilly white apron.

I had found my costume at last.

Chapter Nineteen

I stared as Gretel stood stretching in the doorway. She was rubbing her eyes and yawning. Although it was the middle of the night, she was wearing the full Gretel costume—which was miles too big.

"Did you go to sleep in that?" I smiled. Somehow, the ugly brown dress and the hideous (very) frilly apron didn't look silly on her at all. They looked adorable.

Gretel nodded shyly. "My sister said I

could pretend to be in a real fairy tale."

"Your sister is right," I agreed. Gretel looked exactly as if she had walked out of the pages of a storybook.

"I think she'd like to meet your pretty bird," said Gretel, pointing at the flamingo, who was resting her beak on my shoulder. "Shall I go and wake her up?"

"No! Not now." I lurched forward before she could go back inside the windmill. It was going to be hard enough to explain to one tiny, sleepy girl what I was doing here at midnight with a giant pink flamingo, let alone her big sister too.

Gretel shrugged. "I saw you flying," she said, yawning again and putting her thumb back in her mouth.

"Did you?" I crouched down lower, hoping she was so sleepy she might think the whole thing had been a dream by morning. "I came here specially to ask you a question," I explained.

"Is it about the dusty thing?" Gretel asked.

"Dusty thing?" Perhaps I hadn't heard her properly. It was hard to understand what she was saying with her thumb in her mouth.

She stuffed her free hand inside the apron pocket. "Look."

My tummy somersaulted as she pulled out the magic jar. "You've got it!" I grinned. "It isn't broken!" But my heart sank as I peered through the cloudy glass. The moth was as gray as ash and barely moving.

"Darkest dungeons!" I gasped. It was as if all the hope inside the jar was fading. Gretel was right. The moth was a dusty thing—dusty, gray, and dying. I remembered the bright, shiny creature Aunt Hemlock had captured when it first flew out of the Ables' chimney.

One thing was for sure: I must have

disappointed the Ables very much if this was all that was left of their shiny hope. The child they had really wished for must have been very different from me.

It felt as if a heavy giant in iron boots were standing on my chest. When I held out my hand, it was shaking. "Please, Gretel," I said. "Can I have the jar back?" Perhaps if I could return the moth to Honeysuckle Cottage, where it came from, the hope would start to shine again.

"Hmm." Gretel stretched out her hand. The little jar was almost in my fingers, when she suddenly stamped her foot. "No! Poor dusty thing . . ."

She popped her thumb out of her mouth, unscrewed the lid, and shook the jar. "Fly away," she cried.

"Stop!" I tried to catch the frail gray creature as it fluttered free and rose into the moonlit

sky like a flake of silver ash above a bonfire.

The flamingo made a desperate grab for it with her beak, but the moth darted sideways. Free from the jar, it seemed to find new strength.

"Now look what you've done!" I cried.

"Oops! Was I naughty?" Gretel's eyes filled with tears.

"No . . . of course not. I'm sorry." I reached out and took the jar from her fingers. How was she to have known that by setting the moth free, the hope it carried would vanish like smoke in the sky? "Go back to bed. This is all just a dream with a pretty pink bird in it," I said. Then I leapt onto the flamingo's back.

I had to catch the moth. "In the morning, just remember to tell the little gray kitten that Bella said goodbye."

"The gray kitten . . . ," said Gretel, yawning. "I wish he had somewhere nice to live." She waved sleepily and stepped back inside.

"So do I," I whispered.

The pale moth was already above the windmill, so there wasn't another moment to lose. I patted the flamingo's neck and held out the jar like a butterfly net.

"Sweep like wings into the sky
Brush the clouds and fly, fly, fly!"

I squeezed my legs against the bird as if I was riding a winged horse. The flamingo shot upward like an arrow.

"There!" I cried as a tiny spark of silver light glowed in the sky. "I can see the moth!"

The flamingo wobbled. Her left wing dipped low, almost hitting the big white sails of the windmill.

"What's the matter?" I asked, wishing for the hundredth time that I could speak Flamingo. But the beautiful pink bird flapped harder, raising her left wing just high enough to rise above the building.

"Well done!" I cheered, but the flamingo was still tilting to one side. She turned her head and snapped at her wing, as if trying to peck away an irritating flea.

"Is this better?" I tried as hard as I could to balance my weight the opposite way. Leaning as far as I dared toward her right wing, I clung to her feathers with one hand and held the empty jar with the other.

"Missed!" I groaned, scooping at the night sky as the silvery moth fluttered just out of reach. I'd have had more luck gathering stardust in a net.

I scooped again. . . .

"Get it!" cried a tiny voice (speaking in fast and fluent Cat Chat). "Let me try. I'll catch it with one paw."

"Rascal!" I gasped as his fluffy gray head appeared among the feathers on the flamingo's wing. "What are you doing there? No wonder the poor flamingo can't balance."

"Mom said I belong to you now," purred Rascal, scrambling up in front of me. The flamingo was able to fly straight again at last. "I've come to help. Aren't you going to catch the moth?"

"I'm trying," I snapped as the moth dived past me again. "This would have been a whole lot easier without a hairy ball of fluff hiding under there."

"No need to hiss," said Rascal. "Kittens are good at catching moths. I'll show you. . . ."

"Stop!" I cried, trying desperately to grab him as he sprang toward the fluttering silver light. "You're going to fall."

It was too late. The tips of my fingers brushed the end of Rascal's fluffy tail. But he was already tumbling through the dark sky.

Chapter Twenty

"Rascal!" I cried. The tiny kitten was falling fast.

The flamingo swooped like a heron diving for a fish. I clung on with my knees—one hand held the precious jar and the other grabbed wildly for Rascal as he plunged beneath us.

We were so low that my feet brushed the earth before I caught him.

"Yowl!" he yelped as I grabbed hold of the

fluff on the scruff of his neck and swung him safely back on board.

"Well done, Flamingo!" I cheered as she rose into the sky. A second slower and the little kitten would have hit the ground for sure. "I'm so sorry I hissed at you, Rascal," I choked, burying my head in his soft fur and hugging him tightly. "I know you were only trying to help."

"Trying?" purred Rascal. "I think I did better than that!"

I looked down and saw he had the fluttering hope moth caught gently between his paws. "Whizzing warlocks, you're amazing!" I scooped the moth into the jar and twisted the lid on tightly. "Thank you, Rascal! You're the best kitten any young witch could hope for. All we have to do now is get the moth home to Honeysuckle Cottage."

Suddenly the flamingo lurched sideways as something cold and slimy hit us in the face.

"Ouch!" I cried.

"What was that?" yelped Rascal. But I knew the feeling at once . . . like being slapped in the mouth by a big wet fish.

"The Curtain of Invisibility," I said. "It is drawn around the Magic Realm. Quick! Turn around."

The flamingo was amazing. She spun like a spider on a pinhead and shot back over the hills of Person World.

"How can something invisible hurt so much?" said Rascal, straightening his crumpled whiskers with his paw.

"I don't know," I laughed, remembering I had thought the very same thing when the Curtain of Invisibility hit me the first time. "Thank goodness we didn't fly right through it." I patted the flamingo's back and shuddered, wondering what would have happened if we had ended up in the Magic Realm. Perhaps we would have been stuck there forever. . . .

"Everything's going to be all right now, isn't it?" Rascal yawned and staggered onto my lap. He curled himself up in a sleepy gray ball. Suddenly he wasn't a brave panther leaping through the sky to save a hope moth; he was just a very tired kitten ready to go home.

"Once we get the jar back to Honeysuckle Cottage, where the Ables are, the magic will start to work again. I am sure of it." I peered through the glass. The moth seemed to be glowing more brightly already. "I might even manage to convince them they want to adopt an inquisitive kitten too," I said, stroking Rascal's ears.

"Of course they'll want me." He yawned.

"I'm adorable." Rascal closed his eyes and began to purr. "The very first thing I'm going to do is catch that big brown rat!"

"My old grumpy wand?" I smiled. "Poor thing. It deserves a bit of peace now that it's free."

I had no idea if Aunty Rose and Uncle Martin would ever agree to having a cat, but I had to try. Rascal had been so loyal and brave. Without him, the hope moth would have been lost for sure.

I spotted the warm orange lights of Merrymeet just ahead. "Hooray for our feathery broomstick, the fabulous flying flamingo!" I cheered. "I promise, I'm going to learn your language so I can thank you properly in your own beak-speak as soon as I possibly can."

Perhaps she understood me already, as she turned her head and nibbled my knee.

"We saved the hope moth! All three of us together. We make a pretty magical team!" I whooped, raising the shimmering jar high in the air as we swooped home over the moonlit rooftops of Merrymeet.

"What's that?" Rascal was suddenly wide-awake. He sprang to his feet, wobbling on the flamingo's narrow neck as he arched his back.

"*Ark!*" squawked the flamingo as Rascal's claws dug in.

I peered over her feathery head and saw that not all the lights below us were warm and yellow. Sharp blue flashes pierced the darkness too. A familiar scream, like a banshee's, filled the air.

"Police Persons." I shuddered as their car roared through the dark streets below with the sirens blaring. "Quick! Let's get home as fast as we can." The flamingo soared over Hawk Hall and skidded to a stop behind the birdbath at the bottom of the Ables' yard.

"Steady," I whispered. Landing a flamingo is a lot harder than flying one. Her skinny legs wobbled like slippery stilts. I slid off her back and rolled over with a bump, hugging the precious jar to my chest.

"Thundering phantoms! That was a close one," I gasped. There was a puff of pink smoke, and the flamingo shot toward the ground like a genie disappearing back into a bottle.

"Yikes!" Rascal darted underneath a bush. "What's happening?"

"It's all right," I laughed. "She's just turning back into a pen. See?" I picked up the plastic feathery pen from the ground. I was fumbling with the slippery jar in my other hand, when I heard somebody calling my name.

"Bella Broomstick! Is that you back there?"

I leapt in the air like a startled frog. The jar slid from my shaking fingers. . . .

Time seemed to stand still.

I watched in horror as the glass hit the edge of the stony path and shattered into a thousand tiny pieces.

Whoosh!

The moth shot into the air like one silver bullet from a gun.

"Wait!" I leapt up, trying to catch it. But I knew it was hopeless. With one last burst of shining light, the tiny speck of magic vanished in the dark sky.

It was over. I had no fast flamingo broomstick ready to jump onto now. This time, the hope moth was gone for good.

Chapter Twenty-One

"Bella Broomstick! Is that you?"

The same angry voice was shouting across the lawn. For a moment I thought it was Aunt Hemlock, it sounded so terrifying and mad. Then I realized it was Aunty Rose. Of course! The magic had faded already. Without a spell on her, she had no reason to be kind and loving to me anymore.

"Bella?" she hollered again.

179

"I'm here," I said, creeping out of the shadows. It was getting light. I glanced over my shoulder and saw Rascal stalking along the edge of the lawn. His tail was twitching as he sniffed the grass.

"Where have you been, young lady?" Aunty Rose was standing outside the front door with her hands on her hips.

"Come here where I can see you," she barked.

I took another step forward into the golden light spilling out over the WELCOME! mat in the open doorway.

Uncle Martin burst through the garden gate. "You found her!" he puffed, running up the path toward Aunty Rose.

"I'm sorry," I whispered. I had ruined everything—not only my dreams, but theirs as well. For once, Aunt Hemlock's magic had been something truly wonderful and good (even if she had never meant it to be). Her cunning spell might have been a trick, but the Ables really had seemed happy to have me before the hope moth was lost.

"'Sorry'? Is that all you've got to say for yourself?" Aunty Rose stormed toward me in her fluffy pink slippers. Tears were streaming down her cheeks. "'Sorry' isn't good enough!"

"I know." I trembled. She must have found out about the spell. "It was wrong. I . . ."

"Don't ever disappear like that again!" Aunty Rose flung her arms around my neck. "We were so worried."

"Worried?" I said. "You . . . you're not mad?"

"You vanished without telling anyone where you'd gone," sighed Aunty Rose, hugging me so tightly that I could barely breathe.

"Typical! Just like my mom," purred Rascal, peeking out from under a bush. "Spitting at me one minute and licking my nose the next."

Slowly, I began to smile. Whatever Aunty Rose did, she certainly wasn't going to lick my nose. But Rascal was right. I remembered how Mrs. Cat had arched her back and hissed at her lost kitten when I first brought him home. Really, she wasn't angry so much as relieved to know he was safe.

"We're not mad," said Uncle Martin gently. "We were just frightened that something had happened to you."

"Imagine how worried we were when we went into your room," Aunty Rose explained. "I only popped my head in to check that you were sleeping soundly. But then your bed was empty . . . and it was the middle of the night . . . and . . ."

"I even called the police," said Uncle Martin as the sirens screeched to a stop on the road outside. "I'd better go and tell them it was a false alarm."

"So . . . so they're not going to arrest me?" I said. "You're not going to send me away?"

"Arrest you?" laughed Uncle Martin.

"Of course not," said Aunty Rose. "This is your home, Bella. You belong here."

"But . . . what about the moth . . . the magic?" I mumbled. My legs were shaking so much they almost gave way beneath me. Nothing made any sense. Why would the Ables want to keep me now that the spell was broken?

"Moth? Magic? Whatever are you talking about?" chuckled Aunty Rose. "There's nothing magic here . . . just warm hearts and a welcoming home."

"But that *is* magic." I grinned. And at last I understood. The Ables wanted me to stay with them . . . and not because Aunt Hemlock had tricked them with a spell.

"You're part of our family, Bella," said Uncle Martin, wrapping a blanket around my shoulders.

There were so many things I wanted to say.

My heart was fluttering
faster than the hope
moth's wings, it was so full
with happiness and love.
But all I could manage was a
sort of gulping sound like a frog. "Thank
you!" I croaked. "I'll be the best child you
could ever hope for."

Aunty Rose shook her head. "Just be
yourself, Bella," she said. "Warts and all."

"Bursting blisters! Have I finally grown
a wart?" I asked, confused.

"No!" laughed Uncle Martin as I rubbed
my nose.

"All I meant is that we're going to get
along fine, just the way we are." Aunty Rose
smiled.

Galloping galaxies! The Ables liked me the
way I was! No magic, no warts, no tricks,
no spells . . . just plain Bella Broomstick.

Chapter Twenty-Two

All the magic tricks were gone, and the Ables still wanted me to stay at Honeysuckle Cottage. I was so happy I could have danced around the dark yard. But Uncle Martin had finished talking to the police, and Aunty Rose was looking stern again.

"There'll be no more wandering off without telling us," she said. "Is that clear? What were you doing out here in the middle of the night anyway?"

"Er . . ." My brain fizzed and popped like a potion. What could I say? I didn't want to lie. Not after I had caused the Ables so much worry and they had been so kind . . . not if we really were going to be a real family. But how could I explain? How could I tell them I had flown through the air on a magic flamingo? How would they feel if they knew they were living with a witch?

"For now," said Uncle Martin, waving to the police as they climbed back into their car, "how about you just tell us the important parts?"

"Well, that's easy!" purred Rascal in Cat Chat as he marched into the middle of the lawn. "Start with me."

And so I did.

"I found this kitten and he needs a home," I said. "The family he belongs to can't look after him anymore. . . ."

"Wait a minute!" I had barely started my story, when Mr. Seymour poked his long, beaky nose through the railings. What did he want now? My fingers twitched on the end of my pink flamingo pen as I thought of the way that he had treated Gretel's family—closing down their bookshop and throwing them out of their home. I wished I could wave my feathery wand and cast a spell on him right now. That would teach him a lesson.

Three Spells That Would Serve Mr. Seymour Right
1: Put warts on his big, nosy nose!

2: Turn <u>him</u> into a windmill.

3: Decorate his boring gray concrete with doodles of cute fluffy kittens (and flamingos) wearing bow ties.

Or perhaps I should simply turn him into a frog (and Piers too, just for fun)!

But this was the Person World, and I had promised myself there would be *NO MORE MAGIC!* I slid the flamingo pen safely behind my ear, where it couldn't do any damage. I would just have to hope that there was some other way I could help Gretel and her family.

"Stop!" Mr. Seymour was waving his arms and jumping up and down. Piers ran out of the house too, wearing his pajamas. I was surprised he didn't sleep in his bow tie.

"Don't let those police officers leave before I have had a chance to speak to them," shouted Mr. Seymour.

My heart froze. Why did Mr. Seymour want to speak to the Police Persons so urgently? Had Piers remembered that I had turned him into a worm? The Police Persons would take me away from the Ables and throw me into jail after all.

"What can we do for you this time, Mr. Seymour?" said the taller Police Person, climbing slowly back out of the car.

"Spotted any flying carpets? Or alien spaceships?" muttered the shorter one, giggling into his sleeve. "Or a witch on a broomstick perhaps?"

The icy panic in my heart was spreading to my fingertips.

Mr. Seymour sniffed. "This may be a joke to you," he said. "But I have called the station three times already. I have seen a—"

"Rat!" screamed Piers as an enormous furry brown creature ran across his yellow velvet slippers.

"Told you, Bella!" screeched Rascal, dashing after it.

There was a flash of brown fur, the swish of a tail, and the wink of a beady black eye as the creature leapt through the railing and scuttled under a bush. I recognized my old grumpy wand!

"Thank you!" I whispered in my best Rat Rattle as the leaves rustled and the end of his thick pink tail disappeared.

"I don't think it's us you need. It's pest control," chuckled the taller Police Person.

Mr. Seymour was hiding inside one of his empty concrete plant pots. The rat had obviously given him quite a shock. It wasn't as good as a Vanishing Spell or giant green warts on the end of his nose, but at least someone had managed to teach him a lesson.

Piers was as white as a ghost too as they both shot back inside their big gray house and slammed the front door behind them.

"Dear, oh dear!" The Police Persons were

giggling loudly as they climbed back into their car. Even Aunty Rose was trying not to smile.

But Uncle Martin was frowning. "Rats in the yard? I don't like that," he said, peering under the bush where the rat had vanished. "They eat birds' eggs, you know."

"What we need," said Aunty Rose, winking at me, "is a cat."

★ ★ ☆

So that is how the four of us—Aunty Rose, Uncle Martin, Rascal, and me—stepped over the WELCOME! mat together . . . and became the family who lives at Honeysuckle Cottage.

Before we went to bed, we all sat at the kitchen table and had a warm drink.

"We'll call this little fellow's family first thing in the morning and tell them we have agreed he can stay here," said Uncle Martin, patting Rascal's head as the kitten pounced on the end of his bathrobe. "I think he knows better than to bother my birds again."

"He most certainly does!" I said, wagging my finger sternly at Rascal. I should have known a big softy like Uncle Martin would be just as kind to a kitten as he was to any other strays (like little lost chicks and me!).

"I wonder what Mr. Seymour was going

to tell the police he saw flying over the village this time," said Aunty Rose, sipping her warm tea.

A dragon?

A flying horse?

A vampire bat?

"I don't know." Uncle Martin shook his head. "But it's the strangest thing. . . . I could swear I spotted a pink flamingo in the sky tonight!"

"A flamingo? Around here?" Aunty Rose raised her eyebrows. "Sometimes I think you must have feathers in that big, bald egghead of yours," she giggled.

Rascal and I looked at each other, but neither of us said a word (not even in Cat Chat).

"He's only teasing you, Bella," said Aunty Rose, "because he knows how much you like that pen of yours."

"I love it!" I said, stroking the soft pink feathers, which were still tucked safely behind my ear. "It's the most magical thing ever to come out of Sellwell Department Store!"

"That's good." Uncle Martin nodded. "You can take the pen to school with you when you start next week."

"School?" I gasped.

"Of course," said Aunty Rose. "Don't look so worried. It's all arranged. First thing on Monday morning, we'll go down to Merrymeet Elementary and meet the head."

"The head!" I shivered, remembering Dr. Rattlebone's bony skull bouncing across the dungeon floor at Creepy Castle.

"You'll make lots of lovely friends," said Aunty Rose. "And you know someone there already."

"Really?" I said, thinking of Gretel's smiley big sister. She looked about the same age as me.

"Piers Seymour will be in your class for sure," chuckled Uncle Martin.

Piers Seymour? That's all I needed.

"Slithering snakes! I'm hopeless at school," I groaned.

But perhaps it would be better in the Person World. And I'll always have Honeysuckle Cottage to come home to.

More magic and mischief from
LOU KUENZLER

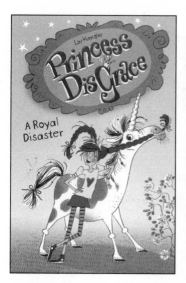

Grace is not graceful or elegant.
Can she prove that being a princess is
about more than just being perfect?

⌒ Collect all the books in the ⌒
Horse Diaries series!

Elska

CATHERINE HAPKA

Illustrated by RUTH SANDERSON

Bell's Star

ALISON HART

Illustrated by RUTH SANDERSON

Koda

PATRICIA HERMES

Illustrated by RUTH SANDERSON

Maestoso Petra

JANE KENDALL

Illustrated by RUTH SANDERSON

Golden Sun

CATHERINE HAPKA

Illustrated by RUTH SANDERSON

Yatimah

CATHERINE HAPKA

Illustrated by RUTH SANDERSON

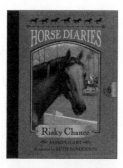

HORSE DIARIES

Risky Chance

ALISON HART
Illustrated by RUTH SANDERSON

HORSE DIARIES

Black Cloud

PATRICIA HERMES

HORSE DIARIES

Tennessee Rose

JANE KENDALL

HORSE DIARIES

Darcy

WHITNEY SANDERSON
Illustrated by RUTH SANDERSON

HORSE DIARIES
Special Edition

Jingle Bells

CATHERINE HAPKA
Illustrated by RUTH SANDERSON

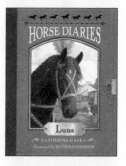

HORSE DIARIES

Luna

CATHERINE HAPKA
Illustrated by RUTH SANDERSON

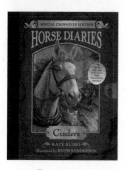

SPECIAL CROSSOVER EDITION

HORSE DIARIES

Cinders

KATE KLIMO
Illustrated by RUTH SANDERSON

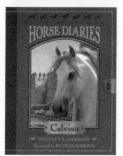

HORSE DIARIES

Calvino

WHITNEY SANDERSON
Illustrated by RUTH SANDERSON

HORSE DIARIES

Lily

WHITNEY SANDERSON
Illustrated by RUTH SANDERSON